Displicit

Displicit

Bob Janis

Writers Club Press

San Jose   New York   Lincoln   Shanghai

Displicit

Writers Club Press
an imprint of iUniverse, Inc.

For information address:
iUniverse, Inc.
5220 S. 16th St., Suite 200
Lincoln, NE 68512
www.iuniverse.com

Cover photo by Claire Sceeny
Cover design by Munish Arora, Bob Janis, and iUniverse.com
Used with permission

ISBN: 0-595-22316-8

Printed in the United States of America

Dedication

◆

Then I said, "O Lord God, cease, I beseech thee! How can Jacob stand? He is so small!"

The Lord repented concerning this; "This also shall not be," said the Lord.

Amos 7:5-6

Dedicated to the ever-changing mind,

and to those who continue to change mine in the most uplifting ways:

my parents, Mark and Janet, my brothers, Matt, Phil, and Ted,
Christopher Warne, and Abbey Dillon

Also, I'd like to thank Claire Sceeny, a great photographer and even better friend; Munish Arora, Alex Sobel, Yugon Kim, Mark Howlin, Ewan Phillips, Andrew McKenna, Jadie Montgomery, and Jeff Rounds, for all the years and beers; the writers' groups, teachers, bookstores, and libraries who have helped me along the road; and finally, iUniverse.com, for letting a schmuck like me do a thing like this.

Contents

◆

Dedication v
Being Dead 1
Mexican Wallet 5
My C. 21
Radiator 23
The Awkward Matter of Kipling 25
So, Where Ya From? 33
Fairy Tale 36
Manhattan and the Mountain 37
In a Hurry 74
The King's Castle 79
Teardrop 87
The Nothing 88
A Letter From Duane 89
Phat Juice 91
Michigan 137
Cat-sitting for Schrödinger 138
Four Mornings 140
Another Day at Oxford 163
One Drink, One Candy 166
Opposing Sides 169
AlivelikeCohen, GoodlikeBukowski 201
About the Author 203

Being Dead

———— ◆ ————

It's no fun being dead
Touch fades as your fingers dissolve into nothing
You slowly begin to dislike your own smell
Rats chew your eyeballs as if they were little
        chocolate bon bons.

But that's not the worst part.

The worst part is being six feet away from anywhere
Like some ineffectual but persistent runaway
        You're always six feet away from home.

I miss the little things, really
I don't miss food I miss the way a peach
        seeps into the corners of your mouth
I don't miss success I miss the gentle voice of a
        friend waking me from a glorious night of sleep
I don't miss fucking I miss the smell of cheap perfume
        as my lips strain to touch another
I don't miss fucking I miss sitting around with Bill
        and the goofball watching the tube and wondering

why we couldn't get laid tonight
I don't miss fucking
    Well, O.K., I do miss fucking—
    It's a little thing really.

And I try to tell myself it's not so bad
    Being dead
It's just like college in a way
I lie around all day feeling queasy and
    thinking I should probably be doing
    something constructive
Except there's nothing constructive to do
It's more like a permanent postgraduate degree
    With a thesis on dirt, dirt, and more dirt
It's more like a hangover with no night before.

I could go to heaven or hell, I suppose
But both seem like they're missing about half
    the people it takes to make a really good party
Both run by the same sick and twisted board of directors
"Anything you want" they say
"Drive a race car six thousand miles per hour"
Ah, yes
And if I crash I'm not even hurt
Not even the least bit scarred
And if you pinch yourself you don't feel it.

And you can't love
No, love isn't eternal
No, no, no, quite the opposite
Love is fighting time every second of the way
Love is a fire lit in a crowded goldfish bowl

Try lighting the same fire in the desert
It's hot but it ain't love.

Regrets I've had a few
And I've got nothing but time to mention them
Getting angry in Aisle Six over the price of Cocoa Puffs
Watching my eighteenth game show because real life
        wouldn't let me buy a vowel
Turning my back on a wonderful friend because it was
        her turn
And she wouldn't follow the rules of fair play
And she was bad for my image, anyway
Bob, Bob you stupid prick
You had it all, and you thought you'd prefer
The stultifying boredom of perfection.

And I worried about the stupidest things
My bank balance, my pride, Alex giving me my GUAR CD back
Man, did I worry.
Job security?
Job fucking security?
Let me tell you something—being dead is job security
Being dead is the ultimate 401K plan
I mean, the dividends aren't great, but the risks
        are so low.

My daughter's worried about dying
I'm already dying, she's thinking
Since birth, every day I've been busy dying
She's right
She is dying, she's right
But if I could talk with her again

And I would trade the company of a million rats
I would throw to the wind the knowledge I craved
     And the peace I cherished
To talk with my daughter again
If I could talk with her again
I would tell her not to worry about dying
She is dying, but dying is fun
Dying is the most uplifting, magical,
     exhilarating thing she will ever experience
It's being dead that ain't no fun.

Mexican Wallet

◆

Natalia Torres knew she was not a pretty girl. Her face was plain, dull; she had dull brown hair, dull, thick, Mexican skin, and dull, fat cheeks. Her skin: too much pigment to be perfect, yet too pallid to be truly interesting. Her whole body in the mirror, Natalia saw that she was a little bit overweight, with just too, too much of her dull skin—or maybe it was too much blood, bone, and fat behind it. She took this all in not with bitterness, but with a grudging acceptance. She was a practical woman.

And she was a happy woman. Not completely satisfied—who can say that—but happy. At thirty-six, she had crossed a lot of ground, and she didn't mind, now, where she was. Sure, she was less young then she used to be, but this was not as bad as some would think it. She could recollect her teenage years without having to dress the memories up in roses, and was grateful for the relative ease of her life now. The little problems that announced their existence each day no longer dominated her thoughts the way they did when Natalia was sixteen.

She had friends, of course. Who doesn't? Most of her friends were guys. Natalia didn't get on with most girls—too petty, pretty, self-centered. She was a person who could have a few beers at *El Gringo*, sit around with her buddies, do almost nothing—totally *relax*. Most girls just couldn't do that. Even if that's what they seemed to be doing,

Natalia always found they were trying to get ahead somehow—impress some guy, probably. Women needed to look out for themselves—Natalia certainly agreed with that fact—but there were times and places for things. Simply *doing nothing* was out of range for most women—motivated girls. Such women, Natalia noted, ended up married but not happy. Natalia would make sure she became both or neither, and expected the latter.

Natalia did nothing best with Benito. Life being as interesting as it occasionally turned out to be, most of Natalia's male friends had slept with her at some time or another, but not Benito. Their friendship was too special for that. They'd get silly drunk together and spend their whole night playing backgammon and making fun of friends and others. Benito could do an impression of lazy-eyed Alfonso (the amiable, stumbling, old man of the neighborhood) that made Natalia laugh every time. Benito and Natalia laughed a lot. To her, Benito *was* laughter—embodied everything Natalia felt and held to be true about it, like some pagan god from long ago. Just the look of him, wearing a half-drunk can of beer and a complicated grin, could set her off.

The wallet lay on the table, imposing. It was worn, had been well used. Stencilled into the brown leather was the word 'Mexico' on one side, and a picture of a Mayan pyramid on the other. Next to the pyramid was a cactus. The contents of the wallet were four thousand eight hundred and seventy-five pesos, an El Paso library card, and the driver's license of Bill Anderson.

Nogales, the town in which Natalia and Benito lived, was on the Mexican side of the Arizona-Mexico border. Its basic reason for existence was to let United States citizens purchase a little of Mexico without having to travel too far past the immigration checkpoints. The dusty streets were swamped each and every day with tourists searching for bargains in blankets, wooden sculptures, and other useless "cultural" bric-a-brac. The items were sturdy enough but nobody really cared much for them. Not the artisans, at any rate—most of the stuff had been crafted at assembly lines in peasant factories in the South. Natalia wondered if the workers who churned out the familiar marionettes still envisioned some hint of soul in each clown and cowboy, as the numbers climbed to the millions. Shopkeepers and beggars competed for the dubious honor of ripping off the foreigners as much as possible. Benito worked for an astute and quiet bespectacled businessman at a shop nearest the border, where the prices were highest and the goods tackiest. Benito loved haggling over prices, and the feeling when he knew someone had bought too high. He wasn't above being a sentimentalist when it came to children and animals, but sympathizing with overspent tourists was beyond the call of duty. "They got money, now I do too. We're in the money club. Same money, same club," was how he put it, chuckling.

Benito never looked like he was working. Slouched against a doorway, he'd yell out to whoever dared walk by the shop without going inside. An innocent acned boy walked by; Benito would yell, "Hey sir! Wanna beer? Wanna girl? I get you a girl." He probably could. Sometimes he even bought the kid a beer, if he bought something expensive.

Natalia waited tables at 'El Gringo', a restaurant deeper in town, just north of the railroad tracks. It served over-greasy food to over-greasy Americans. 'El Gringo' had probably been named as a joke, but it must have been a clever one, because the tourists took a liking to it. The Americans never cared much if you made fun of them. It only reasserted their casual sense of superiority. Mexicans were a likeable subspecies to them, filthy, in dead-end lives—interesting to look at, nice folk, and worthy of their pity. Natalia checked herself and stopped thinking so uncharitably. They were all right, Americans. The worst of them were fat and stupid and rich and self-important—in other words, no different from some Mexicans she knew.

Bill Anderson was more than just American—he was from Texas. He was a businessman of some sort. He didn't wear a ten-gallon hat, but Natalia could picture him in one. He was chubby, like herself, forty-three, with a ruddy complexion and fair green eyes. He was a head taller than Natalia, and it was a nice head—a delicate curve at the upper cheek, just by his ear; a nose that blended in well with his other features; a fragile but full-lipped smile. From his corner seat at El Gringo, two days ago, Bill ordered the chicken enchilada and a Corona.

Natalia was assigned Bill's table. She asked why he was alone.

"Well, ah'm from Texas, but ah'm visiting mah parents in Tucson. Ah came here for the day to git away from them."

"Why, senor?" Natalia knew American and could say 'man', 'sir' or 'dude'—depending on the circumstances, of course. But she had to say 'senor' to the customers; it was restaurant policy.

Bill smiled quickly and continued. "Well, ah love them, gawd knows ah do, but after a while they're just too much. Just too much hassle, you know what ah mean?"

"I understand, senor."

Throughout his meal, they traded nice words about their respective jobs, lives, and countries. It was all pretty straightforward: Natalia was in need of some sex, and she could tell he was in the same boat. Bill's Corona and the two Dos Equis Natalia had tossed back during her break made for plain sailing. Obviously, Bill wasn't going to stay in Mexico, but Natalia wouldn't have wanted him to, either. To be frank, he didn't look like the type that was going to steal her heart like in a Hollywood movie, but he was nice enough and she had had a few beers, and the Hollywood life could surely wait until tomorrow.

Natalia had heard of the idea of the 'game of love' but never understood whether lovers were meant to be teammates or rivals. The evidence didn't quite support either option. Clearly, however, they were both waiting for a move to be made, and at the end of the meal Bill made it.

"It sure is too bad ah've got to go home. Ah really do love your town."

"So why don't you stay?" She countered. "Your parents?"

"Well, no, ah'm sure they'd be jist as happy without me for a night. But ah don't know anybody here—excepting yehself, of course."

"Don't worry about that, senor. Come along, there's a party at my friend's house tonight. This is your chance to see Nogales! And I will find you a place to stay, no problem." Both knew what that meant. But she wasn't going to go so far as to recommend her place—not yet. As things stood, she could still change her mind, put Bill up at a hotel, if for any reason he turned out to be a disaster on two legs.

They went straight there. The party, if you could call it that, was at José's. What passed for a party at thirty-six was far from the vision of an eighteen-year-old. Half the crowd—all people Natalia knew vaguely or well—were sat at one end of the room, watching videos, and the other half were more or less dancing to Mexican chart and the best of Bob Marley. A table was loaded up with *chilli rellenos*, chimichangas, and fried ice cream for snacks. And two balloons—Natalia didn't know why anyone would bother—lurked like awkward losers on the periphery of the makeshift dance floor.

Bill didn't dance, so they sat on the couch. Already, the party was beginning to seem like a bad idea. They'd talk during the boring bits of Saturday Night Fever, dubbed. Though it was all boring to Bill, who didn't speak Spanish, beyond 'Hola', 'Buenos Dias', and '¿Cuanto?'. Natalia would have liked to blame the language barrier for the lack of discussion between her and her date, but the truth was that there were more obstacles between them than mere words. It seemed like everything they had to say to each other had been said at the restaurant—and that was all small talk, waiting-for-the-bus sort of nonsense. Natalia was sure that there were selections from Bill's life and thought that she'd be interested in, but she had no means by which to uncover them.

Bill was clearly made to feel awkward by all the locals, who shared their opinion of the Texan with Natalia in brazen Spanish. Themes ranged from dislike to distrust—"He's too quiet," and "He looks like a jerk. Ditch him." This was an old ritual among their social circle—the disparagement of someone's romantic interest, accomplished little by little, in snipes and glances. It wasn't pretty, but its purpose was to reassure Natalia, stressing that they would never judge her, their old friend, by the future actions of this untested intruder. Every new lover got the same treatment by the group, even the good-looking ones, until they had proved themselves to be good boyfriend material. Natalia knew that Bill would never get the opportunity to make things right with them, and so, even if he never did anything wrong, Natalia's friends would blame him for the one-night stand, and he would be the subject of malicious gossip for weeks or even months to come. Since people generally liked Natalia and would not want to perceive her as a slut, she would be seen as a victim of her own misguided yet understandable urges. *You have to go through a lot to sleep with someone these days,* Natalia thought.

Bill didn't ask what they were talking about. He fidgeted with his bola, swallowed his food after two or three desultory chews, and tried to make sense of Spanish Saturday Night Fever. José, ever the gentleman, sat down on the other side of Bill and made polite conversation. Natalia liked José. Everyone did. José was one of those nice people who are so nice you feel obliged to overlook the fact that he's a little bit dull. What he lacked in edge he more than made up for in other ways. Natalia couldn't count the predicaments that José had guided her through—an overheating Buick, a frantic last-minute shoe shopping trip, a conflict between date and babysitting and so on—and he, of course, was too kind to keep a tally. She had slept with him many years ago, a year or two after they had becomes friends. It was one of those things that went from being a terrible secret to a fabulous joke within a couple of months. Predictably, he was caring and sweet in bed but didn't move the earth for her. He would have tried to, though, had she only asked.

Natalia took advantage of José and Bill's conversation, and walked to the bathroom. She had intended to use the event as an excuse to mingle with the rest of her friends, but upon rising from the sofa, decided against it. There would be too many questions, too many comments to deal with. She glanced over at Benito, who was chugging beers while prattling loudly with Rolando and Marcos. Benito, she knew, had assessed what was going on with her and the stranger, and was already dreaming up the mock haranguing to which, at the earliest opportunity, he would subject her. Well, he would have to wait.

She went to the bathroom and smartened herself up in the mirror. She tried to look uncritically at her reflection, but focused instead on the tiny wrinkles forming under her eyes. While Natalia knew men too well to be overly impressed by them, and thus was not entirely shocked by the fact that a man found her attractive, it was, nevertheless, a pleasant experience, looking at her face in the mirror and thinking, *someone wants to have this, to be near it.* She tucked a few stray hairs behind her ears, reconfirmed her makeup, and stepped back out into the main room.

Natalia stopped outside the bathroom door, and scanned the assemblage, getting a good look at every person, in turn, more to waste time than anything else. *We're an old bunch now,* she thought. In their wild years, when they'd go down to the river to shoot pistols at old tires, when they'd party in the Baja clubs and beaches until sunup then drive home in no fit state, in those years there had been the feeling that anything could happen—even if they didn't know what that meant, if they didn't know what anything could be, beyond the basic sins of sex, substances, and dangerous living. Now, thought Natalia, eyeing Clara, recently a mother for the third time around, who was fawning over Ramon's new Labrador, anything would not happen. They knew what would happen: children, raising children, and more work, work, work. Sex and drugs might happen; danger, thankfully, was no longer such a thrill; but as for anything, that was not even a dream these days.

As Natalia returned to the scene, José was talking to Bill about e-business. José was in marketing, but Bill knew little about the subject and was plainly having to feign interest. Natalia sat back down by Bill's side and gave him a warm smile. In a funny way, she felt closer to him after walking to the bathroom and back. She had looked across the crowded room and found Bill, skin pale amongst the caramel faces, and had discovered an affinity, based on nothing more than wanting to be together for a moment or two.

"You like it here?"

Bill seemed taken aback by this simple question, but he quickly recovered. "Sure."

"They are nice people. Most of them, anyway." Natalia laughed to make sure she got the point across that she was joking.

"Yeah, they're nice folk."

"You want any food?"

"Naaaw." Bill patted his stomach. "Got more'n enough here anyways."

Natalia laughed again, at his joke this time. "Tell me," she said, "what you like about Mexico."

"Well, that there's a tough question. First of all, it was the partying. Went to Cancun on spring break, and…you know, usual stuff. But then—see, we got a guy in our company. Mexican fella—legal, totally legal—and he works *hard*. Works his ass off, if you'll pardon mah French. But he's a nice guy, too, you know? And ah giss…ah giss America could learn a whole lot from that."

"That's very interesting," Natalia said—although privately, she wondered how much the U.S. could really learn from some guy in Bill's company.

She felt a bit sorry for bringing Bill to José's party. It was hard for him. Whenever he spoke to Natalia, all ears listened.

Worse yet was Benito, the bastard. He refused to leave them alone. Benito spoke English well, but when harassing Bill, adopted a deep Mexican accent.

"So, Beell," he'd slur, "a-what do you theenk of Mehico? Too many Mehicans?" Then he'd laugh.

Or, "So, Beell, a-what do you theenk of Natalia? She ees pretty, no?" And he'd laugh.

Or, holding her jaw like a possessive aunt, "So, Beell, wouldn't you joost lurve to keess thees face here? I would, but I am joost her amigo. So don't you worry." Again, laughter.

He sounded like a Mexican out of an American cowboy film. When he got bored of that approach, he became an American out of an American cowboy film. As Bill walked to and from the food and drinks table, Benito would assault him with either, "Howdy pardner," or "Ello, amigo." Bill smiled uncomfortably or didn't respond. Natalia was very upset at Benito, and he knew he would hear from her later. She had invited Bill here, so this was a transitive slight against her. Benito knew how she felt about this, but couldn't resist.

By the end of the night, plenty of beers had been had and life was running smoothly. Bill and Natalia remained on the sofa—not touching, except for an occasional hint of elbow, but sharing a comfortable slouch. Bill asked if he knew a place where he could get some sleep. For a moment, Natalia worried that he was actually looking to get out of the situation, but alcohol helped her to conquer such thoughts. She told him he could sleep at her place, if he wanted. He said okay. To Natalia's great relief, everyone pretended not to notice as they shuffled towards the door. Then Benito's gruff voice called out.

"Natalia!" The goat-fucker.

"Natalia! Come here a minute." Benito was sitting alone, his chair beside a small card-table José had pushed against the wall to make room for the party.

"Wait one second please," Natalia said to Bill, curt, furious, and polite. She steamed towards Benito.

Just before she began yelling at him, Benito said, "Hey." It was a quiet word, said under his breath, with a kindness that was intentionally in contrast to the way he had just addressed her, and it stalled her momentarily. "Have fun tonight." There was a pause. Benito smiled. "Go for it. What the fuck—it's only sex." He was a sweetheart, really, Benito.

Bill and Natalia walked home in the warm night. Bill was more at ease then, his natural bravado not threatened by foreigners. They talked about disco, where they were in the seventies. Natalia was in Nogales, dancing and singing and shoplifting. Bill was at college at Texas A & M, doing something similar. Except he didn't dance, or sing, or shoplift—but he did drink, and yell, and vandalise. The two old rebels had since cut down to dancing and drinking, respectively. The funny thing was Bill was part of the Christian Fellowship. Natalia considered herself a pretty devout Catholic—she tried, anyway, had drunk and tasted Him—but she hadn't seen faith in Bill. She asked about his religiousness.

"Oh ah believe in the whole nahne yards ah do. Jesus Christ the lawd our savior. Not that I'm bragging, you understand. You may be a Catholic, I may be a bahptist—but we come from the same place, ah do believe."

Natalia was not sure if they came from the same place.

She put the key in the door and slowly turned it. The bolt slid and the door opened. Soon came the moment of truth—intimacy would begin to escalate until it reached a point where she could not hope to control it. If she did opt for control, the night would end with Natalia on her bed, and Bill, disappointed but (she prayed) polite, sleeping on the sofa. Or she could succumb to her instincts and make her and Bill both feel good, at least for a little while. She wondered what was really the right thing to do.

Natalia's apartment was very tidy. One room had a table, a TV, a couch, and a bookshelf, one room was a kitchen, one room was a bathroom, and then there was her bedroom. The bed had flowered sheets on top of which, neatly folded, was a Mexican blanket.

"So ah giss ah'm sleeping on the couch," Bill said.

Natalia looked into his eyes, said nothing. Silence could hint so much while committing her to so little. She relished that contrast, between the unknown and the felt, which gives silence its sex appeal.

Natalia's heart sped up slightly each beat. He fumbled towards her, touched her naked forearm with the tips of his fingers, leant in and kissed her. His tongue gave a little at her touch and his breath smelt of beer. Man's breath and beer: a familiar taste to Natalia, mixed with a comfortable warmth.

Before long, unfamiliar hands touched familiar places. They went to the bed, lay down. She ran a hand quickly along his front; he was already hard. That potential awkwardness out of the way, Natalia continued, determined to enjoy herself.

They were soon naked and close to fucking. This was as much Natalia's doing as it was Bill's. She sensed his hurry and was eager to please him. Of course, many women look out for their own needs first, just as a man does. But Natalia had long ago determined that that didn't make her happy. Whether it was outlook or just the way things were, her happiness was dependent on other people, whether she liked them or not. *I'm a born waitress*, Natalia thought.

She directed him to a condom underneath her dresser—hopefully not past the sell-by date, it had been so long, and it was too late to check now—and they got right to it. She leaned back, sighed, felt him near and touching and within her, felt rapture, intense and complete, as it pushed all the complicated details from her mind. He wasn't too bad—he could more or less go through the motions, and Natalia felt joyously active within mind and body.

It was all over pretty soon, and neither minded too much. Bill had cum quietly, being the heavy breather type. Natalia threw in the odd groan, but she hadn't cum. She didn't often.

It was all just an action, a sport. Benito knew it, Natalia knew it, Bill knew it—it seemed as if they were all sharing some joke fit for thirteen-year-olds. Natalia felt that somewhere, sex had a spirit, which could rise up out of all of that heaving and grunting and make it beautiful. But she hadn't quite found it yet.

It was in the quiet after that she was most happy. That was true togetherness, even more than sex. Bill was a good sleeping friend, a big teddy bear. Even though neither fell asleep immediately, they didn't talk, and Natalia liked that. Silence was their common language, and could be beautiful to hear.

Bill left in the morning. While she wasn't attached to him, Natalia allowed herself the playful wish that Bill, in a moment of romance, had proposed to her. She'd have said no, of course, but she would have liked to be flattered. For all she knew, Bill had a wife, but that didn't need to affect her ridiculous fantasies. However, Bill wasn't being ridiculous that morning. He left courteously after they both awoke. Natalia made sure she said "good-bye" and not "see you": it was important to be straightforward at times like these.

Natalia went to work. She walked along the Avenue Obregón and thought it odd how, a handful of hours before, Bill had walked towards the same restaurant on the same street. She had never seen him on Obregón, and she never would. But they shared this road, had both seen the brick buildings and the dust, had felt the same heat. They both owned it in memory, and Natalia, lifelong local though she was, would not begrudge him that possession.

At lunch, Sanchez, the short order cook, had some jokes prepared about 'Wil' Bill Hickock'. This cheered Natalia up. Things never seemed so serious when Sanchez's huge form loomed into perspective.

In the afternoon she found the wallet. He had left it by the bed. It must have dropped out of his pocket. She looked at it, examined the contents. She would have to send it back—the thing created a small amount of trouble for her, and that was all. The post office was already shut. She put it on the table, went to Benito's.

It was time to see him. How could she have a romantic encounter without his afterword? Benito was her emotional midwife—he brought out whatever was inside of her, made sure it survived and she did. She had told him this metaphor many times before, and he always countered with: "Nati, do I look like a chubby old lady?" Which Natalia assured him that he looked exactly like.

Benito lived in a large house with his two sisters' families and his parents. She gave the door a knock. Benito appeared, wearing a ten-gallon hat. Heaven knows where he had found it.

"Hi there, cowboy," he said, in exaggerated English. Then, in his own tongue, he added, "How was your *ranchero*? Did you ride him like a horse?"

For some reason, it was all too much for Natalia. She felt tears in her eyes and on her cheeks. She hated to be a little girl and cry about nothing, so she tried to wipe the mess away with her hands.

Benito knew he had overstepped the mark. He took off his hat.

"Natalia, I'm so sorry. What happened? What did he do?"

"Nothing. No, it's not like that. I'm sorry. I don't know, maybe I'm just feeling bad about last night." Even as she said it, she knew it was not true, not exactly. The thought of Bill alone did not arouse such feelings in her. No, it was a complicated cry, involving many shades of many people, and much about Natalia herself, most of which would never be brought to light.

Benito cooked for Natalia, despite the many protests of Benito's mother, who wanted the honor for herself. After a brief verbal scuffle, she relented, and went upstairs and carry on with her sewing, perhaps sensing, in the way that only old women can sense these things, that the two kids needed to talk.

Benito made *chilaquiles*, a dish he loved to cook morning, afternoon and night, without regard for tradition. While he burnt the chilies and the garlic, Natalie told him every detail between El Gringo and her apartment, from her first words to Bill up until her first kiss with him. Benito wanted to hear all of it, and more, but Natalie never went too far into carnal details, even with her girlfriends.

The food was ready on the table, untouched, before Natalia finished her narrative. As Natalia polished off the final tidbits of her tale, Benito sat back in his chair with a satisfied expression, as if he had already ate well.

"So how do you feel about it?" he asked.

"Not bad," said Natalia. "It's all over and done with now, I suppose."

"Did you get his phone number?"

"Only because I got his wallet." Natalia hadn't planned on telling Benito this, but she hadn't quite set her mind on not telling him, either.

"Natalia! How crafty of you!"

"No, stupid. He left it there, by accident."

"Any money?" asked Benito, grinning.

"None for you," said Natalia.

"You mean you won't share with your friend?"

Natalia reached into her soup and hurled a soggy tortilla chip at Benito. "I have to send it back, you idiot. What kind of prostitute do you think I am?"

"A poor one? A friendly one, who always shares her money with her pimp?"

Natalia knew better than to take him seriously; he was far too predictable to be offensive. They cleaned up and then played backgammon. Benito threw sixes and talked trash. Natalia never could determine how he got away with it all.

She was in a good mood as she returned from Benito's. However, glancing into the familiar rooms of her apartment, a curious malaise afflicted her. Her surroundings were the same but they weren't so much hers anymore. The whole front room seemed nothing more than a frame for the wallet. Natalia did not know what her problem was. She went to bed.

A night went by slowly. Natalia felt it pass, like a train with a long, sad whistle.

Natalia lay in bed as the day started. The wallet was there as the light began and there as the light grew stronger. Bill's Mexican wallet. The light gave definition to the creases in the old leather. He had never said he'd been to Mexico before. But she had never asked if he'd been to Mexico before. Four thousand pesos was more than enough money for a hotel. She had known he could afford a hotel, why was she thinking like this?

She got out of bed and held the wallet in her hands. Sending back was the right thing to do, and so she would do it. He had done nothing wrong to her, was a nice guy. The driver's license said, "18 Ballard Way, El Paso, Texas, 08751."

She heard a sound from the street. Benito was yelling an indistinct something in his hoarse, vigorous voice. Her friend and the whole world were outside in the sunshine. The wallet seemed smaller now, only a trinket, a worthless relic from her distant past. She smiled.

Natalia Torres put four thousand eight hundred and seventy-five pesos into her pocket, and walked out the door, into the heat.

My C.

———————◆———————

There is something about her
As her hips slip
Out of her whispery smooth sarong
Her pillowcase tummy bare and a little cold
And she smiles in a way I don't know how
As if she's telling me she's right here
Yes she's right here
She brushes fire against my skin

(I never said, "You have a beautiful cunt"
I never said, "I love you"
I never said, "Let me nibble your delicate stomach"
I never said, "Tonight I will take you to a little stream we will both discover
                and burn leaves there in honor of what we may have"
I never said, "I hate you in a thousand cherished ways as ribbons on my
                heart"
I never said, "No please please don't go and then maybe I won't have to
                miss you")

One hand across her waist
Her eyes turn softly to me

Purring a glance
The feel of a breezy day
Along my fingertips
A tiredness that we share at this hour
Her bed lightly gives way
As a cotton bud irons a kiss against my lips

(I never offered to give her children
I never smashed my fist into her mirror
I never woke her up with a muddy daffodil
I never drank from a cup delicately balanced upon her foot
I never told all her secrets to a man at the pharmacy
I never gave her a star wrapped in fairy eyelashes
I never called her and asked her to come back
I never wanted her more than I could restrain
She will never read this poem)

Radiator

◆

I sit, one shoulder hard against the radiator, the taste of last night's uncooked shrimp still hanging from my tongue

(and love is stronger than the sycamores taller than the ancient forests huge, and love is greater than the electric storm and more durable than time)

Billy Bragg's voice partially covers the noise of Pop FM and the construction work being done upstairs

(and love is bolder than the tiger and faster than the jet, and love conquers all things as water seeps into cardboard)

My head is half-cocked and the shivers of heat negotiate their way through my limpness

(and love is finer than a sunny day and brighter than a lightning strike, and love cannot be stopped by the heaviest boulder)

I'm waiting to get a call back from a shitty job that may be my future; waiting for a date on Thursday with a girl I don't much care for

(and love is the mistress of all things the stirrer of fate, and love is more powerful than all this crazy world)

The Awkward Matter of Kipling

◆

That morning I met the dawn. A careless streak of blue and yellow against the darkened sky. I had been waking later and later, and the dawn rising earlier and earlier, and on that morning our schedules intersected. As a consequence of this change in hour—mine, not the dawn's—I would lose the Billingham contract. It would go to Farnsworth instead. I had wanted to get Billingham, because it would have meant a rather good-looking bonus when all was said and done. But at least I was catching up on my sleep.

I walked along the country path towards the train station. I hurried along at a fast half-run, half-walk, but when I heard, through the trees, the train arrive, and shortly thereafter depart again, I slowed down. The next train was not for another thirty-five minutes. I would be late. I knew then that I would lose the Billingham contract, that Salynte would give it to Farnsworth. There was nothing I could do.

Resigned to my fate, I walked along the dark green lushness of my neighborhood. I tried to remember my dreams from the night before. I had had no dreams. A peaceful night. I turned my thoughts to Billingham again, but didn't want to waste my own time imagining my smarmy, well-oiled employer dropping into the eager hands of my compatriot Farnsworth what, given the proper combination of dedication and circumstance, could have been mine. So I quickly changed subjects again, and considered the awkward question of who killed Kipling.

Kipling had been found dead yesterday morning by my wife. Blood on the neck and head. My wife wasn't sure if death had occurred during the night, or on the previous day. She couldn't be absolutely sure that Kipling *was* entirely dead—the thought lingered in her mind that it could, in fact, be merely in a coma. She failed to convince anyone in the immediate vicinity to take an interest, and so had to wrap Kipling in a bag, and take it to the vet's herself.

The vet, after making her wait three-quarters of an hour on account of a sneezing Chihuahua, pronounced Kipling an entirely dead cat. Blows to the head with a sharpish object, possibly a garden hoe. My wife was devastated. She drove Kipling home and buried it, under an unadorned white cross, in the front garden.

I didn't kill Kipling, but I can't say I was sad to see it go. The creature was my wife's idea, and my mistake. One impetuous day I caved in and, knowing my wife's unfulfilled predilection for things feline, fetched the ginger kitten from a pet store. My wife called it Kipling—after an exceedingly good cake, I can only surmise. She was thrilled about this new member of the household. I was also much loved but could neither purr nor prowl.

I soon regretted my purchase. Kipling was not as clean as could be expected of a cat, and often smelled of feces. My wife ignored this fact and told me I was imagining things. This is not the sort of thing one could imagine even if it were desired, but I did not argue. I merely stayed out of Kipling's way, and Kipling, all credit to the effluvium on legs, returned the favor with regards to myself. Our well-confined mutual dislike was an agreeable arrangement to us both. We were both madly in love with my wife, but we didn't compete for her affection. It was simpler to just pick different times of the day to express it. I secured early evenings and breakfast; Kipling, in turn, approached my wife only during the day, while I worked, and late at night, while I slept. In this way we saw as little of each other, and as much of my wife, as convenience would allow.

On time, the train arrived, but too late for me. I embarked nonetheless.

The cat and I were on common terms of non-endearment until winter forced us to reconsider our positions. Kipling, apparently unaware of its naturally appropriate coat of fur, refused to venture outside. At times it would take a few cautious steps out into the brisk air, only to abruptly turn its tail and run inside. I was unhappy with this alteration in behavior. The cat, along with the uncomfortable fragrance that accompanied him, was always indoors. Specifically, it was always in close proximity to my wife. My only hours with my true love were pilfered by an overly domesticated animal.

Of course, to my wife's perspective the solution was simple. All that was required of me was that I share her company with the putrescent individual, and chat about the day's events with my wife while Kipling was *aussi chez nous*. I hasten to add that I did attempt this. Removing any mention of the noxious odor from my conversation—for I could not remove it from my mind—I spent many an hour with my life companion, playing Scrabble, cooking, convalescing, and so on. Which is to say, all the merry activities we used to carry out perfectly satisfactorily as a mere twosome. To these activities Kipling appeared to contribute nothing, merely complaining of its incessant hunger and giving off its unpleasantly unique aroma. Yet still my wife insisted that the cat was wonderful to have around.

But one evening the stench became unbearable. I was holding my wife's hand as Kipling lay across her lap, my wife regaling me with an entertaining anecdote involving the son of a librarian whom we knew. My enjoyment of the tale was tempered only by the ever-present reek of

said cat. Yet I persevered. At one point, my wife was getting to a particularly amusing section of the story, and upon hearing a certain quirk of
the fellow in question I chuckled with unfettered glee. My laugh was
considerable enough to induce within my person a sharp intake of air.

I couldn't help but smell Kipling. The beast's unsubtle suggestions of
defecation overpowered my every atom. The smell traveled from my
nose immediately through to the deepest recesses of my brain. My very
being jerked with the sheer horror of the moment.

It would be fair to say I lost my cool. 'Will you get that damn cat out
of my sight', is a phrase not dissimilar to my remarks. I stood up while
saying this, presumably in an attempt to maximize the impact of my
pronouncement while, at the same time, moving my head further away
from the painful scent.

My wife, understandably, was upset. I had interrupted her story and
insulted her cat. Without saying a word she ran out of the house, paus-
ing only to remove her jacket from its hook by the door, and, before I
could make any intelligible protest, she was gone.

Kipling and I were alone. Disconsolate from my wife's departure, I
didn't so much as glance at the life-like ball of fur in the corner.
Although no look passed between my eyes and Kipling's, I could sense
that the cat, ruffled that my outburst had caused its mistress to abandon
it, didn't look at me either. We inhabited the same house and each
other's thoughts—if indeed the mistreated neurons that rattled around
in its empty head could rightly be called thoughts—but to an outside
observer we would have seemed worlds apart. We both pottered about,
engaged in meaningless, distracting tasks. I fiddled with the radio dial,
hoping to find something suitable for ten minutes' listening, even as I
knew there hadn't been anything worth listening to on the radio for at
least a decade. As for Kipling—yes, I caught a glimpse of it now,
through my own continued misfortune—Kipling's tongue licked its
paw, which in turn stroked the fur on the back of its head, a combination of actions that Kipling must have thought had some slight bearing

on the world. Perhaps it was trying to do something about the stink. I silently applauded Kipling's attempts, but I doubted all the licking in the world would make much of a difference.

The train lurched monstrously to a halt. It stopped for about a minute and a half, a transgression on my time neither fathomable to myself nor about to be explained by anyone else. Finally, the engine sputtered sadly and began its toil again.

I had no idea of how long my wife might be away. It was not wholly beyond the realm of possibility that she might return within minutes. On the other hand, the abominable reflection of having been yelled at by me might lead her to spend the night at a friend's house. Thinking this, it occurred to me that the company of a friend might be just what I needed as well. I picked up the phone and dialed Robert.

Robert must have had little planned for the evening, for upon hearing my request he said he'd be right over. This news cheered me up immensely. I absentmindedly polished our better set of silverware, and before long the doorbell rang. It could well have been my wife, but upon opening the door, I discerned that Robert had arrived. I shook his hand warmly and invited him inside. Robert assented to an herbal tea, which I then made. We sat across from each other and shared our reflections on our separate recent experiences. I explained about the current situation with my wife, to his kind sympathies. The time was busy passing happily when the doorbell rang again. My wife!

I opened the door to a drenched, unkempt, and yet utterly beautiful vision. She had been walking in the rain. My wife brushed by me without a word. She swept herself into the bathroom to dry her hair. When she emerged, her tongue was vitriolic. Specifically, she wanted to know why I had invited Robert this evening.

I found this out of keeping with good taste, particularly as Robert was in the room at the time. While I know that my wife has some vague distaste for Robert that she's never managed to put down to anything specific, she had always gone so far as to be civil. Robert, kindhearted soul that he is, got up to go, but I protested. Were Robert to leave now, he would, I am sure, spend the rest of the evening thinking he had somehow overstepped the mark, merely by coming to our house when I had asked it of him. I wanted him to know he was welcome here.

It was far from desire and intention that I berate my wife, but berate her I did. I was very angry. My wife gave me a look that could have frozen gin and stormed upstairs. The cat, loyal as always, ran in her wake. Robert looked on pityingly as I sank slowly into a chair, and the ground adamantly refused to swallow me up.

At last, the train arrived at the spot which I would have wanted it to occupy three-quarters of an hour ago. A short walk, and then my work-day would begin.

It was while I was sitting in my chair that a curious thing occurred. The cat came back down the stairs. It approached my general area with a quizzical expression on its face. Upon reaching my feet it paused for a moment then leapt into my lap. I was stunned. This was the first time, save the obligatory pat on the head in the pet shop, that there had been contact between us. I was nearly gagging on the odor. I could somehow feel the pungent waves catch on the furthest portion of my throat. Under normal circumstances I would have swatted this noxious entity off of my person, but the extent of my shock was such that I did noth-ing. I just stared at it.

Kipling paced on my thighs, its tiny claws piercing my trousers and the extreme layers of my skin. It brushed its body against my chest, bringing it even closer to my nose. Still I did not move. Finally it curled up upon me and rested its head against my knee. Once it had settled, Kipling raised its head and looked directly into my eyes. Its look told me everything, and I was furious. I instantly knew what Kipling was doing. It was gloating.

The shock of Kipling's outright gall hit me like a physical assault. I jerked my knees up involuntarily, causing Kipling to yell and then leap to the ground. Before it did so, however, it scratched its paws deep into my leg, drawing blood through my trousers. In an instant the creature was up the stairs. It probably had a mind to inform my wife of my latest act of mistreatment, but without the proper vocal apparati it couldn't begin to raise a whisper. I was left with a crimson scratch on my leg, a bewildered friend in my armchair, and the lingering scent of Kipling's last stool. I don't know if I have ever felt so awful in my life.

Robert, feeling himself to be incapable of any assistance with regard to myself, motioned to leave. I dissuaded him from this course of action. It would not be quite true to claim that I had a plan, because plans exply reasoned thoughts prior to events, and at this stage I needed no thought and could act without them. I turned to Robert and had a short, frank discussion. I asked him if, as a favor, he could come by the house tomorrow and take care of the cat. I would supply him with a key. I wanted to take my wife out to dinner, and the idea that our smug feline friend would join us was not attractive. I realized I was taking advantage of Robert's friendship, so I offered to do something in return, if I could be of use. Robert assured me he'd be happy to help.

Work. I approached the door that I had opened on so many prior mornings. I opened it once more, and began my ascent of the stairs to my office.

The next morning, my wife, after much cajoling, agreed to let me make amends in my way. I spent the day at work blissful, due to the opportunity the evening would present me to change my wife's dour mood. Sure enough, that supper was a night I'll always remember. The food was superb, the company all I've ever wanted, and the cat was barely mentioned. We drove home as if in the same delicious dream.

When we arrived at our home, Kipling was not to be seen. This was a cause of some agitation in my wife, as she could not remember letting it out of the house. She walked into the night and called its name, though Kipling never seemed to respond to such prompting at the best of times. I assuaged her fears by commenting that wine was having the effect that wine was unfortunately prone to do, and so not to worry unduly and take things out of proportion. She was still perturbed, but felt tired, so took my assurances as excuse enough to take us to bed.

The day after all this my wife found Kipling under a shrub.

At the door to my office Robert Farnsworth greeted me and shook my hand. He said he was sorry I was late, but I don't think he was—and, for that matter, neither was I.

So, Where Ya From?

———————◆———————

I come from a kid's gluestick heart
I come from the everywhere ocean
I come from the bones that didn't crack.
I come from the peasants' kiss
I come from the loosely cobbled road, grating hard against bare
      feet
I come from the uncertain growl of a coyote
I come from the rolling hills of a Jersey dump
I come from the thought of lemonade on a too hot day
I come from Xerox and Xerox and Xerox
I come from the deconstructed apostle
I come from far out dude central
I come from hi-frequency Alabama radio
I come from Confucius says
I come from the moon, now
I come from the tired legs of Salome
I come from the word America
I come from the hungry prowling gavel
I come from the a priori hangover
I come from second base with no one two men out
I come from the wireless phone call

I come from the silences of Auchwitz and Birkenau
I come from plastic and cellophane
I come from the still statues of a hundred gods
I come from the empty difference between peach and brown
I come from the first bonjour on a fifth grader's tongue
I come from one making two
I come from two making another
I come from the children's sound of seashell sea
I come from the temples of Allah
I come from the ferret's choice of toilet
I come from the field no longer fallow
I come from a leaf falling on an old man's head
I come from a dime spared
I come from the new first look at something that isn't water
I come from Helen's lipstick
I come from the Styrofoam surrounding a Quarter Pounder with
      Cheese
I come from hopes never happened
I come from the stories of old women
I come from the happiest day in July
I come from wet dreams of Tutankhamen
I come from the guy who just didn't quit
I come from the final potato
I come from the letter not written too late
I come from the misdirected photon
I come from the honest gaze across the dance hall
I come from nothing up his sleeve
I come from the kindest word in Babylon
I come from the general store
I come from Tom Joad and Sancho Paza
I come from the last gasp
I come from the drums of Africa

I come from the warning of red
I come from the epic clipping of a toenail
I come from the graffiti in the Galleria dell' Accademia
I come from medically proven fiction
I come from the monstrous winter, the evil clawing winter
I come from a seagull's patience and impatience
I come from the 12-hour waitress at the 24-hour diner
I come from three thousand specks of dust on the mantelpiece
I come from my mother and father

I come from life,
from death,
from the sound of jazz and flowers,
from the reverberations of a whisper.

Fairy Tale

◆

Once there was this boy[1]. He met[2] a girl, and they[3] fell in love[4]. They lived happily ever after[5]. The end[6].

---

1 He's twenty-one now, and he's gained a couple of pounds and a bachelor's degree, which I guess qualifies him for 'man' status. Though he confesses to feeling that not much else has changed, so perhaps he was a man then. Unless he's a boy now. Unless it doesn't matter.

2 Well, she was in the same room as him and a bunch of mutual friends. To be honest, he didn't really notice her much at first, even when Sandra and David and Jake said they were so perfect for each other (being, as they were, almost equally good at Ludo) they should get married.

3 And that, I think, is the most wonderful thing. Not 'he and she', but 'they'. Like Melvin said yesterday while helping to count out the cash register, you know it's a true friend when you can feel free to say nothing in their presence. Of our couple, I can tell you that often they'd say nothing for hours, or at least long minutes, at a time. Sometimes he'd not even think about it. On very rare, beautiful occasions, he wasn't there—they were there. Behind a field at a summer concert they said nothing as the sun went down. But he ruined it, because he kept thinking about how he wanted to kiss her.

4 Asher was always critical of the helplessness of falling in love, and, in return for many a delicious omelet, this footnote goes out in his honor. Let's say they 'swam in love': surrounded, they were lifted up by it, but only if they knew the proper strokes and breathing—which, fortunately, comes naturally to most of us.

5 Though not, I'm sad to report, together. They meet up with each other from time to time, to discuss how their lives are going, to say hi, etc., etc. The time between meetings gets longer and longer. And, if you must know, the boy's not exactly happy: actually he plays countless games of Minesweeper in a daze, and needs all his courage just to wake up. But this is my fairy tale—I mean to say, I wrote it—so give me a break, okay?

6 She's studying to become a social worker, or possibly a teacher; he's currently unemployed.

Manhattan and the Mountain

◆

New Jersey Turnpike, Thursday, 9:23 am: I'll never make it big in New York, now, and all because I went to Washington instead. A lurch in my midsection. Just past the George Washington Bridge. Going South. Heart, maybe, or stomach, I'm not sure which.

There's no way I missed it. New York. I was only half asleep. It's too big, takes too long to go through. But it's undeniable. The Empire State is getting smaller and smaller. We are pulling away from New York. At sixty miles per hour. A mile a minute. I take deep breaths to slow down my heart.

How could I have been such an idiot. In the wee hours, 5:45, Hartford, Union Station. Not checking the front of the Greyhound before I got on it. But I was tired. And I like to think quick there, at Union Station, Hartford, site of my mugging (another story), site of the Christians (ditto). And now, site of my unwanted DC trip. Quick, but not well. How many busses leave that accurs'd isle at 5:45 in the morning? At least two, it turns out.

Thinking back. The ticket check girl. Black, with huge orange nails on her left hand only. Coiled around her fingertips like pieces of orange peel. Not a typical beauty. I don't mean black and beautiful. There's nothing atypical there. But the asymmetry. Symmetry is typically beautiful. All colors of symmetry. That's what they say. I heard her tell two

Jamaicans, father and son perhaps, Gate #1. I heard nothing of New York. Here's the thing. Where else would two Jamaicans go? To Washington, it turns out. Or Philadelphia, Trenton, anyplace under and beyond New York, city closest to heaven and hell.

The other passengers look unperturbed. Presumably because they are on the right bus. Once, I thought I was on a train going to Greenford, England. Half-hour journey. I was on a train bound for Greenley, England. Nine-hour journey. This slowly became apparent. I saw a man open *War and Peace* to Page 1, and light a cigar. Had to quibble with four different conductors, on three different trains, to make it back to London. Absolutely true. Though the bit about *War and Peace*, I think, I made up later in a drinking story. Much more true than the past. Drinking stories. Can happen again, for one thing.

I thought everybody who was anybody lived in New York. So who are all these people? Maybe I could make it in Washington. Is that where we're going? Make what? I start an internship at 10:00 in SoHo. Would have started. My big chance, fame and fortune, country kid does good. Suburb kid, more accurately. They don't write memorable stories about us suburb kids. Even we don't know any. I won't get there. Not on time, certainly. Now, first bus back from D.C. I could ask the driver to turn around. Old man, stopped after the toll plaza to pee. Everyone stared at him as he loped down the aisle. We all heard him tinkle. Poor thing. No point in asking. He won't turn around. What must be done will be done. Oedipus goes through with his stabbing. I go to DC. Fate's never wrong. As it happens.

I could do it. I really could. Kickstart the fairy tale. Move to D.C., because that's where the bus took me. But I am not a traveler from once upon a time. I'm a Philosophy graduate from the suburbs. Think of the call home, to my family. Think of what I'd have to say. That I got on the wrong bus, embarrassing enough. That I'm staying in the wrong city, practically inexplicable.

Who knows. I might end up in Louisiana, after all. I'm not going to Louisiana because of New York. Because of the phone call. A week ago today. I remember it as if it were now: the phone rings. And rings again. Another ring. I pick it up. John's on the line. I don't yet know who John is. Just a voice on the line. While he's talking, I pace the wood in my heavy-soled Hush Puppies. It's hard to talk on the phone. To strangers, particularly. I'm not there. He's not here. So where are we?

John is from Friedman Films. Or so he tells me. He has my résumé. This frightens me. I don't like my résumé. It's a nasty piece of work. It just sits on my computer and reminds me of my sins and inadequacies. I try not to let other people see it.

But it gets worse. John isn't satisfied with having my résumé. He wants to interview me. There is a position for which he is considering me. Some sort of internship. Oh, great.

I know how this happened. But we have to go back. Several weeks ago, there was a night. Involving tequila slammers. Me and a bottle of Jose Cuervo. And a lime, and some salt. Just felt like it. Like my room-mate back in college. This one night we all went to the pub. Except him. He stayed home and watched himself get drunk in the mirror. I don't know why he did this. But I always wanted to try. Hence, the tequila. And the lime, and the salt. Though I give up on the lime and the salt after a while. Kept going with the tequila, though, as I remember. Although I don't remember much. Just the first few.

And the next morning. Woke up on the tiles. Drool coagulating beside me. My hotmail account and my résumé were both open. I didn't know where I had applied myself. Except to the bathroom floor.

Too good to turn down. I tell John I'll show first thing tomorrow for the interview. So I've got that an opportunity in New York City. Drat. I was actually looking forward to continued unemployment. Tomorrow was going to be the beginning of some rest in my life. Some more quantity time with my girlfriend. Abbey and I were planning to take a couple of weeks. Head down to Louisiana. My grandparents have a place there.

But there's no business like show business. And I need a business. Because there's no money like any money. My bank statement has told me that my cash flow is drying up. My grandparents were going to spot me the gas money to Louisiana. And back from Louisiana. And most everything in between. But I'm broke now, and I'll be more broke after. There's a chance that this internship might lead to money. Serious, New York, film business money. So let's get on with the show.

I call Abbey and tell her the good news. About us not going to Louisiana. If things go well. She tries to congratulate me on the (possible) job, and console the two of us on (possibly) the loss of our vacation. It's a funny feeling. She is thrilled and disappointed. I don't know what to feel.

I don't know whether to sleep or be sick. Can't do either—just fidget to give myself some action. Are these Washington people? Man in a plain black ball cap. Woman who looks slightly off, neither pretty nor ugly nor in between. Blacks, not that I'm prejudiced (although I of course admit that I am, as we all are). The old man, stoic face forward, now finished peeing. I hate his position, relative to me. For these few seconds, not a broad hate but complete. He is God, uncaring and functional. And he doesn't function all that well.

The bus driver turns around. Lincoln Tunnel, from New Jersey. This vessel is bound for New York! Oh char-bless'd tunnel! Let's call it heaven. I am reborn. Back from the dead. Worse, New Jersey. Garden State, my ass. Sing it again, Frankie. New York. New York.

Still, I'm late. Late on the first day, such an obvious no-no. The outsider, the rich kid from Connecticut. Late, cares not for his own valuable opportunity. What will John make of me? What a stupid morning this is turning itself into. I'll have to hop frantically on subway cars, push past the throngs, run down streets that others take taxis on. These vagabond shoes are in a hurry. Traffic stopped, of course. A long time through little Lincoln. Inside the endless concrete, nothing but metal, lights, people, and smoke. A tunnel to a single destination, overstuffed with cars for decades straight. We edge forward for reasons we cannot see, surrounded by numberless repeated instances of us.

Friedman Films, Thursday, 6:15 pm: Bob Janis, New York film person. For that am I. I make an edit on the rape singer footage. My first ever edit. On my first ever day in the business. A two-second shot, between other two-second shots. It's the face of a black girl. I think Jake chose her because she's black. In a sense, affirmative action. I wonder if this is a little too P.C. even for my taste. By too P.C.: I mean not going far enough. What I mean by not going far enough. Being anxious to pay lip service to something, which therefore precludes you from kissing it. Jakob Friedman, producer at Nightline.

Jakob Friedman, who helped bring Eminem and Ted Koppel together. On the screen. I'm sitting at the wicker table when I interviewed there. A knock at the door and I pull it open. I'm being helpful, aren't I? An older—not too old—gent with a bicycle helmet and a way about him. "Are you being helped." Note the period, brash eccentricity. I am, my interview's next. But I'm not stupid. "Are you Jakob Friedman?" A bit too brusquely. He says he is. Looking at the mail amassed on the table, "Have you been looking at this?" I say no. Polite, courteous, not intrusive. "Oh, lack of initiative. That's not a good sign." He's only playing with me. "Are you in school now?" Etc. My answers aren't good. I give him a particularly dull version of my life. A vacant, bored look drifts loosely across his face. He's only playing with me. I tell him it's nice to meet him—what obsequious drivel—and he turns the coffee grinder on in the middle of the sentence. He fucking hates me.

Because of Jakob Friedman there's now some black faces in between the rape singer. Reaction shots. Of when she makes a joke in introducing herself. Of when she first starts singing. Of when it turns out the song is about rape. None of the reaction shots are really from the time we insert them. The magic of television. In fact, most of the girls we insert are actually looking bored and indifferent. The way all schoolkids look bored or indifferent, when they are in school. But when we slow it down on the computer every head move becomes poignant. A girl going to sleep is a girl averting her eyes in sadness. A girl staring blankly, with a blink, is a girl contemplating the horrible.

An edited world is a better world. In some way, under certain circumstances. In a certain light. Edited, (to a) better world. Otherwise, why? Why not just keep it the same?

In the tiny editing room. Me, Meghan, Thomas, John. On the screen. Lil' Sweetie. The rape singer herself. Huge, lovely, bubbly, white, laughing New Yorker. Big, big accent, bigger personality. She was raped as a young girl. She wrote a song about it. Now, she shares her experience with inner-city children at an inner-city school. For charity. We taped it for charity, too. Also, hopefully, for a cable special. HBO, maybe, or Oxygen. 'Feel-good' stuff.

What John says. Though don't get him wrong, he loves Sweetie to bits and loves hanging out with her (meaning: he knows her and wants you to know it): do we think the fact that she was raped affected her body image? Thomas says it must have done. Meghan and I, the newer interns, sit meekly in the midst of our silence.

The whole kit and caboodle. Jake is in charge. The editing department. John heads this, under Jake's supervision. It is John who tells us what to do. In theory. It is really John who pitches his movie while we sit around and look enterprising. In practice. John's movie is about the punks and transvestites who make up the late night New York music scene. It's a great-looking movie. John spends his days telling people this fact on the telephone, while the boring aspects of his job vie for his attention. Spreadsheets, clients, tangled wires. The battle of life versus art. John is a beautiful man, putting together a movie about music. This is an easy battle for him, emotionally. I showed up panting, half an hour late this morning. John was two blocks away. Getting his breakfast.

But he works for his art. On his own time. Sleeping on floors, in bars and nightclubs, and often not at all. He always has a camera in his bag and his bag is always with him. Four hundred hours of footage over four years. A ninety-seven minute movie. Still too long, says John. John told me at the interview I was patient. Patted my shoulder.

An intern was running around, looking for a videocassette. Like a chicken. Worried about its head. She'll never find it. The office serves as the final resting place for thousands of unknown videocassettes. They find their way behind CPUs, or under lunch menus. Her name was Meghan. Is Meghan, in actual fact. I didn't know that then. Because nobody introduced me to the interns. Least of all the interns themselves.

She is beautiful and looks nervous. The videocassette is lost and cannot be found. She is not responsible for the loss of the videocassette. John is not blaming her for the loss of the videocassette. Yet the loss of the videocassette appears to be the primary concern of Meghan's life. This is because the task of recovering the videocassette has been delegated to Meghan, and Meghan is very serious about her tasks. She wants things delegated to her. Her hopes and dreams depend upon it. Perhaps something of importance, perhaps something to do with a movie, the substance of a movie, will be delegated to her one day. And on that day she will pick up that thing and run with it. And only she knows how far she will go. Any day could be that day. Very serious.

John, on the other hand, isn't quite so serious about anything. He was an intern, too. Back in the day. Everyone was an intern once. He likes the whole idea of having interns, now that he isn't one. I sense he is both amused and pleased that I have shown up to the interview in a suit. The other intern applicants have shown up in nice casual. Nice clothes for college kids. Which most of them are. Or barely out of college. They don't know the value of a suit. They don't think film work counts as suit work. It's too cool to be suit work. They think. But I know better. As sure as a suit. Few things, in this world, are. And there is no such thing as suit work. There is only bad work and better work. If I look out of place, it is to my credit. John gives me an interested look and I know I've got the job.

The door opens. Jake, at last, has a moment. A moment to spare for us. He reviews the latest draft of the rape singer footage. He says nothing until it's finished. If you didn't know him better, you'd think he was just watching TV.

Jakob Friedman is a genius. Everyone who knows his work agrees on this. What he does best, better than anyone, is tell the truth. A documentary filmmaker. This morning, talking with one of his producers about her project. She is doing a film on AIDS. One of her interviewees is about to die. She is not sure she wants to film it. She's not sure it's respectful. Of course you will, says Joe. He is right. Instantly, the matter becomes clear. It is not a matter of money, or ratings, or respect. It is simply what she does. She is a documentary filmmaker. She films the things that happen. She tells the truth.

Jake Friedman is not ashamed of the truth. He has chronicled the lives of his old lovers and the deaths of his own parents. Three doors down from where we are working on the rape singer is Mike. Mike, an assistant editor, has been working there for three days. He is editing Jake's proctology exam. Jake has asked him to do this. Mike said he has seen more of his boss's butt in the last three days than he ever cared to see of anyone's, his own included.

But there's no business like it. No business I know. After the interview, I take the elevator down to the street. Down fourteen floors. There's a black gentleman who sits in the lobby. He watches the people go in and go out. That's his job. He needs to tell the right people from the wrong people. I'm not sure how he does this. But it doesn't matter. I'm one of the right people. I step outside.

Hoodlums straddle benches in a tiny sidewalk park. Bike messengers hurtle through lights turning red. Vagrants sleep, stretched over chessboard tables. Buildings, immense, flex their steeled muscled at each other. It's a beautiful day. I belong here. Amongst all of this. A New Yorker.

I walk across the street to the subway. I am going to Abbey's house tonight. So I won't tarry here. I start thinking of the story. The story of today. What I will tell her. What to take out, what to leave in. Important alterations. How should I make Meghan? Pretty, certainly. For one thing, she is pretty. Also, we want to avoid ugly characters. Unless they are interestingly ugly. And quiet. But that's the only read I got off her. So as for personality, I'll have to make one up. Plus, these buildings need to be taller.

Jakob tells me he likes the edit. Which means the edit will stay in. Possibly. Maybe Jake changes his mind. Maybe Lil' Sweetie doesn't like it. Maybe Ted Koppel stops by for lunch, and, in his opinion, the cut doesn't really 'fly'. But that's okay. That's all a part of the business. The business that I'm in.

Famous Ray's Famous Original Pizza, Thursday, 10:35 p.m.: This restaurant's idea of interior decoration. A sign instructing on how to enforce the Heimlich maneuver, with illustrations. Still, I've got two pieces of greasy pizza, a Dr. Pepper, and a place to spend a little time. Very expensive, New York. What you're paying for. A coordination of place and time, especially at night. It's costly to be indoors at night. 24-hour city. At several bucks an hour. Some examples. Bookstores, if you're lucky, but there's few, and they're all closed by twelve. This place cost me $3.75. Two slices and a Dr. Pepper. I'll stay maybe twenty minutes. It'll feel like more, the way they stare at me. Their only customer, scruffily hunched over a crumpled napkin with a cheap pen.

A real restaurant costs over $20, for scant more time. A coffee shop costs some less, and lasts some more. I like coffee shops. I don't much like coffee. I love caffeine's vital functions in society. In the morning (delineate day, awake, alive. Celebrate it. Like an overeager lapdog's tongue proclaim it). The teakettle (the gentle self-sufficiency of friendship. An affirmation). The diner black coffee (Familiar journey into night, the long highway). Coffee doesn't ease hunger or thirst. This is what is good about coffee. It doesn't feed something that will, after all, only return. It just gives you a good kick and lets you go.

Almost no more money left now. Twenty-five dollars for the hostel, plus ten dollars key deposit. I return the key, they return ten dollars. I understand why they take it, not why they give it back. I'd rather have ten dollars than a damn key. A growing desperation. And all I have to look at is a poster of the Heimlich maneuver.

Whereas, a week ago. In Vermont. In Brattleboro. The correct appearance of sushi. Now there's a poster. Tuna. Salmon. Eel. Swordfish. All raw. All wrapped in seaweed. Fresh from the ocean. Food, long before you eat it. Before you cook it. And long before it's removed from your throat via quick thrusts to the stomach.

The waitress is young and looks vaguely happy. In the way all waitresses do. But only vaguely. I forget her name. I let Abbey order for me. We are on the road, in an unfamiliar sushi restaurant. Having unfamiliar sushi. I never liked sushi. Until I decided to. That was five minutes ago, outside the restaurant. Well, we were hungry, and I decided to enjoy it.

Abbey chooses some sushi rolls and two miso soups. Then we talk. Abbey and I. There is a conversation between us. I don't remember what it is about. I'm sure it hasn't been forgotten. It's probably something we still talk about. Our conversation is a work in progress. A changing whole. We love to talk. If we have nothing new to say, we bring back something old. Reinforce our oral canon. Talk can illuminate truths. Bring the mind to new heights. But it doesn't always do that. It also massages the mind's knotted shoulders. We treat it lightly. But it's important stuff. This talk, between us. Nothing can be fully destroyed. Until it is forgotten.

So if there are, let's say, about fifteen minutes between order and food. As is customary. We use them to talk. Once, in France, with my family, in a restaurant. A man with a walrus moustache, and his wife, a small, immaculately nondescript woman. Two tables over. The restaurant was not crowded. Just us and them, on that particular evening. And the waiter. Who wasn't vaguely happy. Not true in France. The happy waitress maxim. They take these things too seriously. Food, and the presentation thereof.

You see, meals in France take a long time. There are many courses. Each course takes a while. The wait between courses, even longer. Our family didn't mind. We love to talk. Stuff our mouths with food from one side and nonsense from the other. The old couple didn't seem to mind either. The wait. They were in no hurry. Seemed not to be. They were not seen to be looking around impatiently. Or tapping their fingers against the tablecloth. They cast mild glances around the room, breathed quietly to themselves, and ate. But they didn't talk. Not all meal, as I remember. Though I'm probably remembering wrong. There may have been the odd 'Pass the croutons' or 'How is it'. In French, of course. But if so, they stood out. Such interruptions to their silence. Stiff and straight. Very dignified. Monsieur Walrus just ate his soup. Madame slurped her snails. With as much dignity as snail-slurping allows. A surprisingly large amount of dignity, I learned.

Abbey and I don't have much by way of dignity. Not our strong point. We use our fingers. Pick up the sushi, plunk it into the pile of wasabi, then grab a tiny strand of ginger between finger and thumb and paste it on. Then we stuff the whole mess into our mouths. Our oral opus of those few minutes. The slurping, burping, bad puns, ridicule, ramblings and chewings.

After our sushi is finished, our bill is paid. Including twenty percent. And I round up. We head back to our car. Let's be honest. Her car. Vermont in March. Too cold for my touch. But I have to. Temperature being what it is. I must touch everywhere. And all the time. An unwilling lecherousness.

Everything's very pretty. The old buildings and the fresh snow. Dare I say quaint. We are in Vermont instead of Louisiana because of the internship. Vermont is closer. Colder, but closer. We only have five days until I have to be in New York. Just enough time. For a quick trek, there and back to Montreal. My idea. A lot of driving involved. I don't mind. Because, by heck, we are going to have fun. Lots of it.

We walk along the street. Which runs along the river. Which runs all the way to near my house in Connecticut. And further to the sea. To the Sound. The Sound of New York.

I have no one to talk to. In the restaurant. In all of New York City. I'm there for eighteen minutes. I know this because I keep checking my watch. Nothing else to do. Not much time. I had wanted to waste more than that. With eating and thinking. But the more I think, the faster I eat. Nothing to do. The pizza restaurant people. Brothers, maybe. But what made me assume that? Just that they're both Middle Eastern? And work in the same pizza place? Or it could be the way they don't talk to each other. They just look at me. Stares, loaded with intent. Intent to what. I don't know. I don't care to ever know. There's a whole city out there, waiting for my input. Once more to the streets.

We are in a bar. With our best friend in the whole world. Or so Larry would have us believe. Judging from the first few minutes of our time together. A big, hairy hippie. Vermont born and bred. Peace, dudes. We don't disagree with him. Ready for another, guys? We each receive a pound on the back. I decline, but get him a beer in return for the round he just bought us. He seems happy with the arrangement. He wanders off. Peace, man. It's a crowded bar. He has many best friends in the place. Some of them from hours or years before our time. Depending on how far back he can remember.

We stopped in here for something to do. It's Saturday night. The whole town is here. It's a small town and a big bar. Still not big enough to fit everybody. But the rest of the folks are more reserved than our pal Larry. We're left alone to talk.

We've said everything there is to say about my upcoming internship. We talk some more about my upcoming internship, anyway. Are you excited? Yes, I am. Yes, it's great to finally 'be in New York'. Yes, it sucks working for free. With Abbey prompting, I babble on contentedly. After that, the relationship.

We don't have a lot of 'relationship talks'. I don't quite know what to say about the two of us being together. I really like it. I hope and think that she does, too. That would explain why the two of us have been together all this time.

I'm not very good at relationships. Abbey doesn't ask me about my exes. She has told me she likes believing she's the first person I've had sex with. Often. Even though she knows it's not true. Which is fine with me. Sex with her is better, anyway.

Abbey's been in some very long relationships. I can't get off my mind what she said on Valentine's Day. We were sitting on her couch, just the two of us. Enjoying the company. I thought it was a good time to trot out the old platitude. About how much it sucks to be alone on Valentine's Day. I guess it would, she said. I couldn't believe her mouth. She hadn't meant to impress me; she just said it. Never a lonely V-Day? Not one? The Valentines I had spent alone. More than I care to remember. It sounded like some sort of legend. The person never alone on Valentine's Day. Not since elementary school.

But it stood to reason. Other people. Finding her as easy to be with as I do. Several long-term relationships. Much longer than three months. Which is my current record. Abbey will break it. A few short weeks from now. All going well. I inform her of this. She finds this surprising. I don't quite understand it either. Lots of different reasons. Me being a jerk. Her being crazy. It just not working. One time, I broke up with a girl because it took her too long to answer the phone. It was my friend's phone, and I was worried about my friend's phone bill. But this one's different. I don't gauge it in terms of love. Love is a poor basis for a relationship. Now, friendship. That's been proven effective. I know. I have friends. And Abbey's a good, good friend of mine. Already. The other girlfriends were much more girls then friends. Strange, inexplicable beings. More to do with me. My perception of them. But now, I'm in love with a friend of mine. And the relationship is on more solid footing. Hopefully.

I don't have a lot of faith in relationships. Abbey says this. It's almost out of nowhere. She started this discussion. I could tell she was leading to something. But I didn't know what. She looks at me for my reaction. On the verge of tears. I see the water forming at her eyes. But I am somewhat relieved. I'm distrustful of relationships. For obvious reasons. My own fault, I know, but that's where I'm at. I tell her how I feel. As best I can.

A couple of phone calls. One to Abbey, to say hi and I love her. Though I use more and different words than that. So who knows what she heard. One to my mother. She's coming to New York with her husband (my father) and her sister (my aunt) on Saturday. After my first two days as an intern. Bob Janis, who has a position in New York City. I'm to meet them at the Empire Hotel, noon. They're coming down early, especially to meet me. Thrilled. Me, them, everyone. I see my parents most days in a month. But in New York, different people. All of them. All of us.

My hostel's booked for one night only, so far. Can stay there all night. Party. But I'm standing at a phone booth. Talking with my mother. Mostly because the hostel's crap. Each floor has a room with a shower and a room with a toilet. No sink. I washed my hands in the shower. Hell knows what I'll do tomorrow. Showering. Toothbrush. Mirror check. There are two bunk beds crammed into my room. Two other young men absolute themselves and pop in and out. The sleeping one. Asian, let's say Japanese, if not American. Has his head on straight. Will wake up early to 'hit the sights'. Not his term. He was too tired to speak with us. The non-sleeping one. European, let's say Czech, could even be American, as he only spoke very briefly. Hello. One word. Two if he said it wrong.

Chelsea is dirty and gorgeous. The sun is long gone and only a sleepy heat remains. Heat from the grates. And the people. Beautiful, ugly, far-fetched, far-flung, fat, ridiculous, ill-fated, fortunate, wonderful, happenstance people, and the dust and soot of all of them falls from them and dances in the air and is broken up and is reincarnated within all of them. And me.

Chelsea is dirty and gorgeous. Everybody's favorite whore. Runs off with your money, your clothes, your very breath. You love her. In spite. If not because.

Fifth Avenue, 7:08 a.m. Morning is a good time. I'm seldom awake. Too bad, because morning is good.

I'm walking uptown. Looking at the places that sell things. Bagel shop. Clothing store, not yet open. Bagel stand. I want a bagel. I can allow myself one, provided it's cheap. Eleven dollars, forty-two cents. After I pay for my room at the hostel. When it opens. Office hours eight a.m. to eight p.m. Tomorrow, twenty-one dollars, forty-two cents. When I get my key deposit back. Minus a bagel. And subway fare, lunch. Etcetera. Call it a buck or two. If I'm lucky.

Morning is a good time. You can feel it. The collective promise of everybody's day. The anxiety adds to the excitement. Gives it bounce. The people in New York City are very busy. Some hustle, some bustle, some both. And most of these people live here! One of the five boroughs, or the richer suburbs. It would be great to live in New York. There must be a million people around here. I'm sure a couple of them must have had extra floor space last night. Instead of my spending twenty-five dollars. A pity. So much, in this busy world, to a lack of communication.

Telling her she's great. That's why I'm in this gas station, buying two ready-made imitation Egg McMuffins. And two coffees. Breakfast in bed. For her, especially. I spoilt the surprise. Kissed her bare back, and told her where I was going. But otherwise, every woman's nightmare. Strange motel room, boyfriend nowhere to be found. The travel dump.

Not that she'd think it. The sex was good last night. Good as in really fucking good. Good as in Jesus and James Brown. There's a bucket of gas station roses. Right by the counter. I throw my food down and add a rose to the pile. Two breakfast specials and a rose. Showing off. I can't read his expression. Guy behind the counter, young, goatee. Looks bored more than anything. So much for jealousy. Well, at least I'll get to tell Abbey. The whole joke. How I bought the rose to brag to a gas station attendant. Don't want to seem *too* sappy.

Uptown to 40th Street. There's an Internet place there. The orange one, Easy Everything. Same as the one in London. Tottenham Court Road. I used to go there, back in my London days. Feeling tired, poor, and huddled. It was open 24 hours, and only cost a pound an hour. I could e-mail all my old friends. It gave me a nice place from which to be homesick.

Ah, London. I miss it now. Streets of London. Hallmark of the champion of pity. Frankie would never sing a song like that. Too pathetic. How can you tell me you're lonely, and say for you that the sun don't shine? New Yorkers and Londoners live in almost the same city. There is one difference. New Yorkers think they live in the greatest place on earth. Londoners, the worst.

Row upon row of orange seats. Mostly empty. I try to remember the truth of the last few days. And what to embellish. And how.

A million miles an hour. We are skiing down the mountain. It is sloped ridiculously. I am very high up. In a few short moments, I will be at the bottom. That's where the crowd of mini-skiers is gathered. Tiny children, six-and seven-year-old, with skis on. This is the fastest I've ever moved without brakes. I'm supposed to be able to bring myself to a complete stop. If I can't, something else will.

If only I had listened to Big Rick. Big Rick suggested we stay on the bunny hill. Learn the basic maneuvers before we try a real slope. Good advice. I can see where he's coming from now. Rick is the one who taught us to ski. That's putting it strongly. As I'm sure Rick would agree.

This is the first time Abbey has ever been in skis. Try number two, for me. The first time, as a kid. I was on the bunny hill. My problem. I could do everything. Except stop. Only way to stop was to fall over. Which I did often. That was as a kid. I'm a grown man, nowadays. Physically, at least. Meaning I fall further.

You have to hand it to Rick. He took pity on us, standing alone by the beginner flag. Abbey with her cigarette. She cuts a funny figure, smoking a cigarette while booted out in ragtag athletic apparel. Like some old-time athlete, from back when athletes looked like real people. Stuff we found in the bargain rack of a skiers' outlet store. I wobble and lurch on my planks. Thirteen years old. That's the last time my feet felt this big.

We're both chickenshit. This is how people break legs. We look up. Everyone's going down. Good skiers and bad. Miles of pure white. Pristineness, interrupted by people. We've just spent an awful lot of money. This was a dare. An unspoken dare. I guess. Nothing else can explain what brings two suburban couch potatoes to an advanced slope in Vermont. Neither of us is thinking about money much. That's the advantage of spending all your money on risking life and limbs. Money can be recuperated pretty quickly. By comparison.

Big Rick starts by telling us to take our skis off. Which we do. Gladly, in my case. Then he tells us how to put our skis back on. The right way. The skis fall off before your legs break. So legend has it.

There are mostly six- and seven-year-olds on the bunny hill. We're not ready to ski there yet. We begin on a gently sloped four-foot mound by the main building. Abbey and I walk up and ski down. One after the other. Rick laughs encouragement at us as we pass. This is fun. He tells us.

I haven't quite figured out the snowplow yet. The method of stopping. Back of skis splayed, front of skis pointed inward. The friction of the V-shape will slow me down, little by little, until I'm stationary. But this is no video game. There are large heavy things on my feet. They don't agree with me. They don't want to splay or point inward. They want to keep going straight. Fortunately, there's only so much steam that can be generated on a four-foot mound. My momentum peters out at the bottom. Then I have to walk back up again. This is another problem. I'm supposed to sort of waddle up. Skis splayed outward. But I keep sliding backwards. Abbey's better at this than me. You have very strong legs, Rick tells Abbey. Do you kick him a lot? Very funny. Abbey laughs loudly. I'm sure I'll hear this joke again. More than a few times.

The tiny children are fast approaching. Relatively speaking. I'm getting closer and closer to the bottom of the mountain. The bottom of the mountain has been tucked beneath the main building. Between my body and the building are a short stretch of snow, and a large crowd of people. Standing in line for the ski lift. Many of them six and seven years old. They all ski better than me. And yet the court would hold me responsible if I ploughed into them. Even accidentally. Crazy world we live in. I could veer left, into the trees. Or right, into the other skiers going down this hill.

Snowplow. Come on, snowplow. My legs can't do it. It feels great. To be going so fast. There's a thrill to it. To not being in control. A release. Like the last moments of sex.

I should have known what was coming. We had been having fun on the bunny hill all day. The mountain loomed over us all that time, daring us, like a naughty older brother. Then I looked at my watch. Quarter of. Last call for the ski lift. I ask Abbey if she wants to. The line for the ski lift is a few feet away from us. The top of the ski lift is out of sight.

Big Rick was nowhere to be seen. He had told us it might be a bad idea. Might be. But I looked at the mountain, and then at Abbey, and I knew we have to do it. I'm not going to end my day on no bunny hill.

The top of the bunny hill may be the best place. To fall over. The forest on my left is about to give way to the bunny hill. Then I can turn left. As long as I don't hit anybody. I try to lean my body in that direction. But I'm cut off. Some jerk. Came out of nowhere. Now he's skiing exactly my speed, right next to me. It's not intentional. His being a jerk. He must think I know how to ski. I'll show him.

Last I saw Abbey. At the top of the hill, snowplowing down. A paragon of grace, she was not. A wounded gazelle, closer to the mark. But she did look like she'll make it down okay. It makes me happy to consider this. In the midst of everything. Suddenly, room. He went faster or I went slower. I turn left. I'm still going too, too fast. I fall. I crumple myself. Become a mess of arms, legs, skis, body. It's really a lot of fun. Feels almost natural. The ground and me, not separated by skis. I tumble for a while, and come to a stop. My skis are off. So are my boots. And hat.

Abbey's further up. Much further. Snowplowing down. Slowly. She's hunched over, looks terrified. I was there. The snow is seeping in and mixing with my sweat. It feels good. Watching my sweetheart reach me. A cup of hot cocoa inside. Waiting for us. I start thinking what we'll talk about. I'll e-mail Chris and Claire in England. Might e-mail Duane, even though the asshole never gets back to me. The best thing about e-mail is how it happens on the same day. Not so serious, that way. Letters often so serious. Letter en route in a carriage, while writer dying in a castle. That sort of thing. A big chunk of my life between sending and receiving. E-mail, often as not, is about tiny slights and momentary glimpses. Better that way. At times.

Keep in touch. But what sort of touch would you like?

New York Subway 'C' Line, Friday, 3:47 p.m.: A pastrami sandwich in the pocket of my overcoat. Cheese and mustard. It will be delicious. I'm sure of it. It's dripping with meat and salt. Dripping through the bread. The smell is dripping through the paper bag. I'm hungry.

I have a very important video to deliver, so I don't eat the sandwich. It's my video. In my hand. The one with my cut on it. Bob Janis, New York film person. It's going to the gays and the lesbians. GLAAD. Gay and Lesbian Alliance Against Defamation. Defamation's very bad. Gays and lesbians are very good. In general. These gays and lesbians are in Midtown.

Construction workers, the same as the old couple. Sitting quietly, enjoying the food. Those hard yellow helmets. All covered in dust and dirt. Just like construction workers anywhere. Except they are daintily sipping their espressos. In the French fashion. Taking their time. This is lunch. Sacred territory.

Abbey and I are in Montreal. The end of the road. Seeing the city after all that driving. It's a nice place. Cobbled streets, French food, construction workers. We have already found a hotel to drop the bags off and are now enjoying lunch. Sizably. One of those all-inclusive menus. So you have no choice but to stay for coffee and dessert. Incentives for the gluttonous and lazy. My kind of place.

After the raspberry tart. We walk out to the end of the pier. There's a Science Center there, and an IMAX theatre. The Science Center is closed for the day. Abbey and I are always late for everything. We live bankers' lives on a nightclub schedule. Don't know who designed this society. The IMAX is showing Everest. Seen it already. We sit on the dock of the bay. Nothing much going on. No ships coming in. No ships going away again. No worries. It's a nice river. I lean over and hug Abbey. God she feels so good. I push my lips into her neck. Her hands hold my arms in place.

Abbey lights a cigarette. She doesn't feel so well. It's starting. The period. My condolences. She doesn't feel all that awful. Just a little tired, and wouldn't mind heading back to the hotel. For a quick nap. A long taxi ride. That's how far the hotel is. We just got here. Haven't done a thing yet. But I don't say any of this. I understand how she feels. Not perfectly. Since I don't suffer from them. Woman troubles. At least, not directly. I just get the fallout. I say it's not a problem. Going back to the hotel. No problem at all.

I don't expect anything like the last hassle. I dropped a video off at Lifetime this morning. The security people. A big black guy in a uniformed red rain slicker, a Hispanic guy in his own clothes. They were bad. When I say bad. Unsatisfying as people. *Qua* people. Unsatisfying to whom. Everyone, generally. On this particular occasion. I don't mean all the time. Just rude. Looked at each other, not me, as they told me I couldn't go up the elevator to see the women. The women at the top. Not so much as a look. Smug in their lowly position of authority. Not that I'm racist. A huge, ugly marble block. Behind them. Some sort of modern art. That's all they had to look at. All day. Hey, I'd be pissed off, too. Just a little respect. That's all I ask. Make believe we're all human. Who knows, it might be true. Evidence to the contrary. They took my video, so I couldn't hand it off to the women the men worked for. But hopefully they will. Hopefully they already did.

The gays and lesbians should be easier. Not that the security guys necessarily aren't. Gay, I mean. Not that it's any of my business. I wouldn't ask them. They'd likely hit me. The gays and lesbians I'm going to see now are people we already know. John knows them, they're nice. According to John. John likes people. Almost everybody. He genuinely does. He gets crushes on fifty-year-olds and admires drag queens. It helps to like everybody, in the film business. Like people a lot. And say so. Otherwise, you have to fake liking people. That gets kind of taxing after a while.

I'm lying with her. She's fast asleep. I'm wide-awake. My arm is around her shoulder. Slowly going dead. I could get a book. Read the guidebook, find something to do for when we wake up. Abbey makes fun of me whenever I pull it out. The guidebook. I love my guidebook. I pore over it at every available opportunity. It's so full of possibilities. Futures. It knows almost everywhere we might go. It's a close call. But I can't quite be bothered to move.

In the taxi. On the way back to bed. This bed. We were speeding down Rue St. Catherine. I was speaking French with the driver. *Ca va?* He could speak English fine. I just wanted to practice. My French is so-so. *Comme ci, comme ca.* Abbey can only speak a few words. She is tired.

She is cranky. She probably wants me to talk to her. In English. *Pas de chance.* She has already taken away my afternoon. Daylight robbery. I drove all this way for a taxi ride and a hotel bed. Not even any sex. I'm being unfair. I know this. It's wrong of me to think what I do. To resent her feeling badly.

But I'm trying to escape. Escape from all my malicious thoughts. And all my malicious thoughts are in English. Which might be why I'm speaking French. A language in which I am innocent. And extremely stupid. The taxi driver soon bores of my French self and reverts to English.

As soon as we hit the bed. I'm starting to relax. I mutter a few consolations at her and she's asleep. I'm awake and doing nothing. Wasting time. Some might say. But I'm also lying in bed with my thoughts, quite near my girlfriend. That's content. I have no other needs at present. We'll wake up in the late evening. Both feeling better. We'll go into the city. Most everything will be closed. We'll have nothing to do, really. It won't matter. Tourist distractions out of the way. Just the important things. Her. Me.

Drips on the video. Drips of pastrami. If there are. On the envelope with the video. Pastrami-smelling drips. Pure catastrophe. Pastrami catastrophe. Good name for a band. Presentation big in this business. Very big. Pastrami less so. This trip is an easy task. Fit for an intern, as they surely say up high. So it pays to be very careful. But I'm daring myself. To get out the sandwich and take a bite. Right here on the subway train. It would drip. Cheese and mustard. Oh yes, it would. But I'm still tempted. The worst thing I can possibly do. Always an attractive option. The Vegas thrill. Risking it all. And losing it. Give up all hope of film world status in pursuit of a pastrami sandwich. Then again. We're talking New York pastrami here.

Southwest Harlem, 10:32 p.m. Nowhere in New York. No place for me to sleep tonight. If only I spent all my money. Checking in, Thursday morning. Booked for two nights, instead of one. Then I wouldn't be in this mess. The girl even asked me. How many nights? I wanted to say two. I hadn't known my parents would come down; I just wanted to chill in Manhattan an extra night. But I was being cheap. I figured I would make friends. Meet someone nice, who'd let me stay at their pad. Always happens in the movies. But when you need something in this town, it won't give it to you. You don't get this much stuff by just giving it away.

So the morning after. This very morning. Eight a.m. sharp. I stood in line to book for another night. That was before the German asked. In front of me in line. Have you any rooms? Formal, like so. They don't have any rooms. Formally or informally. None for him, so none for me. I don't even ask.

After work, I go straight to the International. After walking around Greenwich Village for a while, dipping into the bookshop and the record store. Then straight there. As straight as I get in New York. A turn here, a stop there. Changing direction to walk down glittery streets. A town with straight streets. Not a very straight town. A great place to deviate.

International Youth Hostel. The biggest fucking dump in the world, according to the guidebook. Only substitute "youth hostel" for "biggest fucking dump". If you want to. I never bother. It has about a thousand rooms, staff who range from surly to non-committal, the fellow unwashed. Young European/Asian travelers. Old European/Asian travelers who still haven't figured out the hang of not being poor. Americans in various states of distress. Very good showers. It costs over thirty dollars so will wash me out. Would have, if they let me in. They do not. Not their fault. Blame the army of losers staying there on a Friday night. Ragtag conscripts of the urge to travel. And he is good to me. My counter person. Tells me to wait until ten, even though the other counter person hisses at him not to say that. As if I can't hear him. Tells me people might cancel. I can sit in the TV room and watch TV I sit in the TV room and watch TV

As I sit down Regis is talking to the celebrity contestant. I don't recognize her. "You're hanging onto your last lifeline." Regis actually says this. Come on. Is that meant to apply to me? Is that someone's idea of a synchronicity? How corny. The correspondence is just too blunt. I can't believe I'm being subjected to this. Last lifeline. I'd never put that in my fiction. But that's the thing about fact. The work of a cut-rate hack, sometimes. Sitting up in the gods. The other celebrities shout out answers to make sure the celebrity contestant gets the questions right. If only real people had it this easy. Who's in my gods? Not Cato Caelin. That's for damn sure.

The $500,000 question. The celebrity isn't sure. None of the celebrities is sure. The helpful yelling has ceased. She thinks it might be 'B'. Does she want to risk it? The celebrity deliberates. Making sure her hands don't conceal her face as she does this. *She* wants to, personally, but this is for charity. Young mentally retarded abused orphans who were damaged by flag burnings. Along those lines. She doesn't want to risk the charity's money. How good of her. Give me a break. Here's an idea. Risk the goddamn money. If it's right, great. If it's wrong, make up the difference. From your own pocket. That's public service, you dumb rich fuck. Tired and cranky. It's been a long day. And I shouldn't talk. I have no money to be charitable with. Only slightly more with which to be uncharitable.

We're looking at a mountain. Mont Royal, the royal mountain, namesake of Montreal. It's a two-inch walk to get there. On the map. Little bit further. In person. We walk. And walk. Along Rue St. Denis. Not so impressive in English. Holy Dennis Street. Past Rue Ste. Catherine, with its cars whizzing this way and that. Past the buildings standing still hour past hour. The buildings obscure our destination.

Abbey asks me if I know the way. Sure, I say, glancing at the guidebook. When we see the big thing again, we head towards it. I don't say that part out loud. It's crisp and chilly. Our limbs are tired. Our heavy clothes add a few pounds while making no attempt to stop the wind from biting. Finally, the mountain reappears. Right in front of us. Just like the map promised. Told you so, I say.

There are steps up. Just as the guidebook says. Problem is, we need to get to them. There is a sloped park between the steps and us. Grassy and pleasant. Claims the guidebook. The guidebook must not come here in the winter. Two choices face us. Three if you count giving up. Which I don't. We can walk on the road. The way of ice. The slippery road winds around a long turn and then reaches the steps. Then there is the more direct approach, straight toward the steps. Over what once was grass. The way of snow. This involves less distance, but is steeper. I choose the way of ice and march ahead. Abbey watches me. My foot slips, and my arms prepare frantically for a fall. No fall. Screw this. Quick change of plan. I trudge up the snow. The wet reaches from my feet to the top of my ankles. I'm wearing sneakers. Snow seeps through my trousers. The cold burrows into my flesh. Just keep moving. I look back. Abbey has decided to follow me. We both mumble curses. I curse the snow. She curses me.

We are half-frozen by the time we reach the stairs. Not too many mountains have stairs. Takes an awful lot of stairs to climb a mountain. Mont Royal is proof of that. And these are not Sunday-driving stairs. These are climb-at-your-own-risk stairs. They are steep; they go more up then back. A thin layer of ice has formed on each. Only one handrail, on the right. A thin layer of ice has formed on that, too. We haul our-selves up the first step, using the handrail to help drag our weight away from the earth. A single step. The journey begins. There are a hundred more, just in this stairway. God knows how many stairways. This is really ill-advised. And I should know. I advised it.

As we walk. A man jogs up past us. More a sprint than a jog. He's wear-ing gym shorts, a T-shirt, and a hat. He doesn't bother with the handrail. Where did he come from? This is no man. It is some demon, straight from the depths of the fitness center. We watch awhile. Soon he is above us.

The college kids aren't so humiliating. They pass us, but more slowly. The whole group of us clinging to the handrail. So their passing is a complex operation. An interchange of hands and forced hugs. More warmth, though, when that happens.

At last. We are at the first landing. Abbey pulls out a cigarette. Abbey and I gasp in smoke and air, respectively. One landing done. An uncertain number of landings to go. A pitiful sight. The two of us. Insignificant against the mountain. The Japanese landscape painters. To them, we are tiny blots of paint. Emotions? Physicality? Our relationship? Pah. Two bits of color. What is that, within the mountain?

I had to watch an hour and thirty-five minutes of television. It's okay, I've had practice. I watch a lot of TV. But when all you're doing is waiting for the clock to turn, you realize just how dull television is. Its ability to eat up time is unparalleled. That's how it helps. The ailing, the sick, the depressed, the bored, the guy waiting for the ten o' clock hostel check. Regis asks a question. A long pause, with music. Regis asks another question. Another musical pause. Regis chitchats. A commercial. Thirty cuts per commercial. Thirty edits. Then another commercial. Sixty shots in a minute. Sixty things on screen. Think of Paleolithic man on a slow hunt. Sixty shots all day. By the time we come back from a commercial break, we've been on two days' hunt. And we are still hungry.

Regis ended over an hour ago. Barbara's about to begin now. 20/20. I'm a little excited because Barbara's one of our people. We've done stuff for her. Things. Some day, I'll find out what. We are just entering a commercial break, and it's 10:00. I'm not waiting until 10:02.

The counter person recognizes me. The mean counter person. The nice one went home. He tells me to wait until twelve. I can sit in the TV room and watch TV. I thank him and walk out.

These are my options. Walk around New York until morning, and then sleep a few hours in the park. Try not to get mugged. Ply myself awake with coffee and food. My hostel money will just about cover it. Or: wait around until twelve. Midnight in South Harlem. Maybe walk down to midtown and back. Or watch Barbara, and an hour or more of somebody else. Or go back to Hartford. Too much to think about.

I start walking. Downtown, that decision's easy. 100th Street and below. To 99th. Apartments, shops. Good, good. Onward. 98th. More apartments and more shops. Fine, fine. Don't get mugged. Look mean. Sneer. 97th. The same again. Okay. Twenty blocks to a mile. Can get in a lot of walking before dawn. The objective isn't walking. The objective is dawn. Tomorrow, tomorrow. I want you, tomorrow. It's only a few very lonely hours away. Until my aunt and parents come to see me. Tired, broke, smelling of street stench without a shower. And, critically, a New Yorker. Twenty blocks per mile. That equals…oh, Hell.

I take a right on 96th and another right on Broadway. Then turn back North. Home. Past Yonkers, past the Bronx. Connecticut. To a state of safety. Not sure how I plan to get there, though. Keep walking for a week or two. Sun on my right in the morning, on my left in the evening. Or, take the 1,9 to the S or the A,C,E, down two floors, Gate 36, then on the bus to Hartford. Provided I have enough for bus fare.

I cross the line. Into three-digit land. Black people. All times of day and night. Hangin' out on street corners. Chillin'. Whatever the word is now. Who are these people. The ones who come up with it. The street wordsmiths. The guardians of our changing tongue. I wonder if anyone, during a conversation, will ever tell me. That they were the first. The first with "bling blingin'". With "holla". Or an elderly, legendary gentleman. The first "mofo". But I never get to meet these people.

We're almost too high. We're at the top. We look down on the city below us. It's pretty. A vast expanse at vast expense. At last. No more steps. Except the same ones, down.

There's a wall all the way around and people are sitting on it. I don't like getting too close. I'm not afraid of heights. Just of falling down them. Abbey has every right to be mad at me. This was entirely my hair-brained scheme. She's having her period. I knew that; she told me yesterday. She should be yelling at me. Actually, she is yelling at me. But she's calling me a big loser and I know that means she's only playing. There's yelling when she's mad at me. And wants me to know it. And then there's yelling when she wants me to know she *should* be mad at me, but she doesn't have it in her right now because she likes me too much. The big fool.

We sit on the steps so Abbey can smoke a cigarette. They are long concrete steps, not steep. There are about ten of them and they lead up to the building with the refreshment stand. We will get a soda and a snack shortly. But there are nine more steps to go. And I'm in no hurry.

I'm not sure what the attraction is. Going up high and looking at cities. It just satisfies something. To be removed. See the overview. The taxi driver on Rue Ste. Catherine. Does he know he's just a part of the view? *Bien sur*, he's been up here. I doubt he's thinking about it, at this exact moment. Everyone who turns a light on. Everyone who puffs smoke. They all contribute. Too small to see. As individuals. I see the mass effect. None of the details. Just all the details, combined.

I look at her. She looks at me. I let her speak first.

"Right, ready to go back down?" I laugh. She puts out her cigarette. I put my arm around her. The blobs of paint don't move noticeably. We'll be here. For a good while.

I'm bored and I'm tired and I'm going home. Back to Hartford, my girlfriend, home. I'm not scared of sleeping on the street. I should be, certainly, but I'm not. I'm too tired to be scared. I just want to fall asleep in the most comfortable place possible. The Greyhound bus seems to be it.

Before I head down to the subway, I see the Dunkin Donuts sign. I'm immediately in the mood for a Dunkin Donut. Not because it'll taste good. Ten P.M. donuts never do. For the familiarity. It's like running into a distant acquaintance at a party where you know no one else. You're instantly good friends. I have a dollar and a half over the price of a bus ticket in my pocket. One donut: sixty-five cents. Money to give muggers, beggars, etc.: eighty-five cents. Not being in New York City at the end of today: priceless.

I feel defeated and exhausted. This place has worn me out. As for my aunt and parents. On the way here in a few hours. It's a shame. Thinking about them touring New York without me. Taking a bus alone, instead of a free ride with family. I feel like New York has won, and I have lost. Not for the first time, I'm a failure.

It's a truly tough donut. I'd throw it out. If I wasn't so hungry. I head down the stairs. A short ride until sleep.

Interstate 91, Saturday, 2:33 am: They go round and round. The wheels on the bus. The lives of each of us, here in the gloom, inside this gray heap. The gathered pilgrims of the 12:15 from Port Authority to Union Station. Everyone going somewhere. For our own reasons. Some, going home. Some, running away from it. Some, just trying to keep moving. Some, last thing at night. Some, first thing in the morning. We share a common tiredness. It blankets us, stretches past the over-oppressive air conditioning to reach us each. The few lights on inside the bus create an eerie grayness, somewhere between dark and nothing. I am curled up tightly. I have two seats to myself. It still isn't enough for all the me there is.

I have slept a little. Mostly curled up with my thoughts. The 12:15 from Port Authority is a very holy place. Nothing but your thoughts and the road.

I'm now squandering my thoughts on logistics. Thoughts about the road. Specifically, the two miles of Asylum Avenue between the bus station and my house. There is the matter of a ride home. I have eighty-five cents. More than enough for a phone call. I don't know whom to call. My parents and aunt are fast asleep. Getting ready to visit me in New York. I don't want to wake them. I still want them to go. My aunt has never been to New York. It's immaterial. Whether or not I'm there. She should go.

I don't want to wake them for a ride home. Not enough sleep. It's not safe to drive on it. Asylum Avenue. I'll walk down it. Downright dangerous. At night, foolhardy. Through the heart of the city. There are a couple of blocks of projects on the way. But when they see a white person this late, they don't bother you. They assume you don't have any money. They think you're just a crazy.

I already made a phone call to Abbey. Collect, from Port Authority. I didn't ask for a ride from her. She lives almost an hour from me. I just did it because I needed to speak with her. I spent all day not talking to people I love. I'd had enough. I just called to hear her say any old thing.

I didn't want to say too much on her nickel. I told her I'm coming home tonight. Maybe we could hang out tomorrow. She told me we could hang out tonight. She said to call her when I get to the bus station.

I'm not going to call her. She would have to drive all that way. Just to take me two miles down the road. And then all I'd do is sleep. That's gratitude for you. I'll save her the trouble. Walk quickly, look crazy, lots of sleep ahead of you. And then, when I'm fully recovered, I'll spend some time with Abbey. Wide awake time. Real quality.

An enormous monument of tackiness. Possibly the world's largest middle-of-nowhere souvenir store. A few miles North of the Canadian border. You can see the sign from the highway. You can see the sign from the moon. 'SOUVENIRS'. Before we go in, Abbey takes my picture against the giant red letters. Arms outstretched, I can barely reach the 'O'.

Not so impressive. On the inside. About twenty rows of items. A bored Canadian teenager working behind the counter. Selling everything from placemats with the Canadian flag, to lighters with the Canadian flag, to temporary tattoos of the Canadian flag. And Cuban cigars, of course. For every contiguous American, the true symbol of Canada.

Abbey is looking for a moose. You can't come back from Canada, she says, without a moose experience. She has never seen one. Not even in zoos. Montreal was utterly moose-less. Also, no moose anywhere in the vicinity of our car. Her car. For which I am grateful. It's a Volvo, sure. But a moose is a moose. Surely a saying in Sweden.

But there is no moose. Stuffed animals get their own section of the gift shop. The stuffed animals are made by a company in New Jersey. Huggafur. Bears, chipmunks, frogs, dogs, cats, rats (well, mice), owls, pigs, even ducks. But strangely, no moose. Someone in the Huggafur administrative offices had callously underestimated moose sales in Canada. Probably hadn't figured on tourists.

I ask Abbey if she wants a stuffed bear, chipmunk, frog, dog, cat, rat (well, mouse), owl, pig, or duck. She does not; she just wants a moose. There are plenty of pictures of moose, on placemats and pencils. With Canadian flag backgrounds, no less. But they don't count. Abbey has seen moose on TV. But not in the flesh. Or fur. Or synthetic fur. Synthetic fur counts. She doesn't even want a stuffed moose. Not to keep. She just doesn't want to leave Canada without a single moose experience.

What I am taking home from Canada. No moose. No tacky souvenirs of any kind. My girlfriend. I took her to Canada, too. That is, a slightly different her. A her that had never been to Canada. Now, she has. And a different me. I had been to Canada before. Just not with her. You can take the girl out of Canada. But you can't take the girl out of the boy's memories of Canada. She will always be there, when I go back to it.

And we know more of each other. There was a time when we knew nothing of each other. Not even her name. Not too long ago. There will be a time when we know as much of each other as we are ever going to know. I think this time will not come soon. Now, somewhere in between. A good time.

It looks like I'm it. Her moose experience. She is browsing through the Canadian flag bumper sticker aisle. Her back to me. Here goes. I put my hands against my head, thumbs in. My hands are now antlers. I lean over, paw the carpet with my hoof, and charge.

She turns just before I run into her. With a shriek and a laugh she jumps into the air. Then she tries to put me in a headlock. After butting her with my horns, I put my arms around her. She hits my chest playfully after we embrace. Still pretending to be mad at me.

The teenaged Canadian stares at us from behind the counter. Hasn't she seen a moose before?

I cast a glance out across the way. On the seats opposite, a young, tired black man. He looks at me, too. Ever so briefly. A glance apiece, and that is all of me for him, and all of him for me. All we will ever know. A picture. A two-second shot. And yet, as much behind that cut, as there is in all of me.

The bus lurches a left into Union Station. We're there. Home. To me, at this point in my life. Give or take a few miles.

While the bus slows down. The driver announces there is no getting up to take luggage down from the overhead rack. A passenger gets up immediately after he says this, and proceeds to take his luggage down from the overhead rack. Big, scary, white guy, well-dressed with a shaved head. Probably lives a normal, mainstream life, and shaved his head to look mean. Or the exact opposite. It's a rather pointless act of rebellion. The other passengers don't so much as look at him. The bus stops with an acute absence of drama. The lights flicker on and off for a couple of ticks and then glare. The passengers rise slowly, subdued, like zombies. We shuffle our entranced bodies single file towards the door and out into the night.

The overhead luggage rebel is trapped at the back of the bus. He tries to nudge forward the huge old lady in front of him with his impatience. She ignores him and brings down her things. One by one from the overhead compartment. Deliberately. I am at the far back of the bus, even further back than the old luggage rebel. But I am not in a rush. I need to wake up fully before I get outside. I'm not home yet. This is not a safe place. People only come here for two reasons. They are going some-where. These people don't bother me. I am one of these people. Then, there are those that want something from those that are going some-where. Thieves, Christians, con men, ticket agents. These are the people that worry me.

If only Paul Bunyan could tell us what to do. But he just stands there, awkward. Forty feet tall. A heroic figure with no role. In the summer, he directs people to the amusement park, right behind him. But this is winter, and the amusement park is closed. Paul just leans on his axe, wielding an uncomfortable grin. He's as lost as we are.

We came to Lake George for something to do. Big mistake. According to the guidebook, Lake George is where New Yorkers go in the summer-time. I wanted to know. Who goes there in the winter? Here's your answer. Nobody. Save for dumb jackasses on their way back to Connecticut.

Also elephants, rhinoceroses, hippos and giraffes. There is a small herd of each behind Paul Bunyan. There are tracks around them. The train is missing, has been put into storage for the winter. They are life-size, but not terribly lifelike. The colors are fake. Simple pastel greens and purples, made for children. Too friendly to be wild. We tightrope walk along the tracks. Pet the animals' metal hinds.

We're getting kind of used to it. Having nothing to do. Abbey takes out a cigarette as we lean against a friendly hippo. The vacation is almost over. Soon, back in the car. Then, all the way home. Home, where the music's playing. Home, where my thoughts escaping. Wigan Train Station. The North of England. They have a plaque up there, com-memorating that it was where Paul Simon wrote the song. While wait-ing for a train to get out of there. Says a lot about Wigan. That they'd put a plaque up. Commemorating some guy who wanted to leave.

Lake George is no Wigan. There are lots of things to do. Just not in the winter. It's spooky. We seem to be stuck inside a collection of fifties' postcards. Pictures of 'good old-fashioned fun'. Amusement park rides, water slides, mini-golf. Hand-painted ice cream signs. Haunted houses. Just no people. You can sense them. The ghosts of all the little children who have been coming here summer after summer. You can hear the silence. The lack of laughing and shrieking, noise. The silence is both eerie and overpowering.

We head down to the water. A two-story sits tour boat next to lake. Out of the water. Out for the season. The water is trying to decide. Whether to be frozen over. Chunks of ice mingle above the water. Just starting to melt.

I put my arm around Abbey and hug her as she smokes a cigarette. I squeeze her against me for warmth. Our warmth. My warmth alone draws me no comfort. It's what we share that matters.

Things are about to change. Spring is coming. Any day now. And my life will be very different tomorrow. In New York City. Starting my film career. There's a short while and a longish drive between then and now. And a few more moments of intimacy, here by the lake.

Abbey puts the extinguished cigarette butt in her pocket. A trash can is visible near the tour boat. Later. For every thing, there is a season. Now, the time of cinnamon and sugar. Now, she returns my hug. The rest of our lives. It's waiting for us, up ahead. For the present moment. Let it wait.

The taxi drivers are looking at me, and thinking about my mother, my friend, or my lover. If one of these is here to pick me up, I'm nobody to them. Otherwise, I'm a fare. No one walks home from here. No one white. They think. But I will.

There are two types of taxi drivers. The legitimates. The illegitimates. The legitimates have some nature of sign affixed to the car, and pick up their fares in an orderly line. The taxi queue. One car after the other. When they are not ferrying passengers they have only two things to do. One of them is wait for passengers. The other is to wait for unauthorized cars to park in front of them in their orderly line. Then they hurl curses. In an orderly line, one curse after the other. The drivers at the front don't pay any attention. They will only be there for a minute or two. Picking someone up. Or dropping someone off. Furthermore, they are the type of drivers who park unauthorized cars in the taxicab lane. They are not frightened off by taxicab curses.

But the legitimates don't hate the ordinary drivers. Not really. Even the ones who park in their way. For a minute or two. They just hurl curses at them for fun. The legitimates' hate is reserved for the charlatans, the scavengers, their unfair competition. The illegitimates.

The illegitimates don't bother with signs on their cars. They don't park their cars in an orderly line. It is sometimes not even their cars. I was taken for a ride in one of them once. My British friend Andy and I. We were approached as soon as we got off the bus by a Hispanic man who asked us if we wanted a taxi. We did want a taxi. By an extraordinary coincidence. This man happened to be a taxi driver. We were in luck, he told us. He would take us all the way home for five dollars.

What made this all the more surprising. I hadn't told him where my home was yet. Perhaps he meant his home. I asked if he knew my street. He did, five dollars. I should have known better. I did know better. I ignored my knowledge. For the sake of curiosity.

Another Hispanic, and a baby carriage. That's what waited for us in his car. Parked in a shady lane near the bus station. The Hispanic was in the passenger seat. He got out and offered to put our luggage in the trunk. He opened the trunk. The baby carriage was inside. The two Hispanics seemed as surprised by this as we were. They squeezed our luggage into the trunk, on top of the folded-up baby carriage.

We started our drive. It was very early on that he started upping the fare. Our driver. "Oh, I didn't know it was this far." Hispanic Riding Shotgun agreed with him. Nobody had told him where we were going. How was he supposed to have preconceptions of how far it was? Five became ten. Ten became twelve. Andy became petrified. I became petrified and angry. Also, curiously, amused. I offered them twelve Canadian.

We had just come back from Toronto. They took this as some sort of insult.

They stopped the car on my street. Not at my house. I had given them a false address, a full two blocks from where I lived. A stranger's house. Let them get the follow-up burglary. I mean, business. We settled on ten. I think they were too bored to argue. They stopped the car.

"Okay, get the gun." Hispanic Riding Shotgun said this to Hispanic Driving. Hearts stopped. Not theirs. The driver laughed. "Don't scare them like that." He apologized to us for his friend's morbid humor. We decided to accept his apology. I tipped them 20%. And I rounded up. Very up. Up to 50%.

Had to hide in the back yard. Somebody else's back yard. Until we were sure they weren't waiting around to follow us home. Took fifteen minutes of lugging our heavy suitcases to get home. And Andy has never, I suspect, fully forgiven me. But it was worth it. A durable experience. I'll take it with me to the old folks' home.

I steel myself, ready to ignore everything they throw at me. Their yells. The legitimate and the illegitimates alike. I stare at my feet and resolutely march ahead. Just don't look. That makes it easier. I keep my head down through one "hey buddy". And another "you want a ride, sir?" I don't dare move my head towards the "you got a dollar?" Probably not offering to drive me home. Then again, just might be. There's also a "Bob". It takes me a second. Another "Bob". I look up. It's Abbey.

Who knows how long she has been waiting here. Just her. She's sitting in her Volvo with the engine running. There's an empty seat beside her. It's mine.

I open the car door and get in. My seat belt tries to restrain me but can't. I lean over and kiss Abbey on the cheek. Also, I close and lock the door. Her cheek feels very warm next to my fingers. Meaning my fingers are very cold. I find a spot on her sweater, just at her shoulder, where I can touch her without freezing her. All this thinking and moving takes a couple of seconds. Accompanied by the passion, the usual passion, the minor permutations in blood pressure on which the whole world turns.

I tell myself to stay awake. After driving all this way, Abbey deserves my consciousness. I begin to drift away. I tell myself to stay awake. Again. And yet again, I begin to drift. I can feel the sleep's comforts pull me gently closer. Farewell, sea of troubles...

The secondhand smoke from Abbey's cigarette gives my heart a tiny jolt and allows me to stay awake a little longer. I have something I need to say. I want to tell her how much I appreciate her picking me up. How much I appreciate everything. All she does for me. All she feels for me. All she is. "Thanks, sweetheart." And another kiss on the cheek. That's all she gets. She gets it. She puts the cigarette in her mouth and her left hand on the wheel, so she can run her right hand through my hair. And they say the days of perilous romance are long dead.

It's no use. I will soon be asleep. My body is beginning to supersede the wishes of my mind. I might just last the car ride. I have a definite plan for tomorrow. Which is today. My agenda: nothing. If that's all right with Abbey. We might just make it out of the house. If not, no bother. I'll tell her about New York. In boring detail. We'll cook. We'll watch TV. We'll make love.

Our only destination, the minute in front of us. How we get there. Eventually.

In a Hurry

◆

I don't think I can take much more of this.
I was walking to the train that takes
me to work and
I was twenty minutes late.
It was a beautiful day, the sun
caressed us each: the buildings, the
concrete, we who will become
sinners and we who are not yet
saints, we felt ourselves against
that bosom of heat, which was
grateful for the life of us and
even might have loved us.
On the way down the hill I see
the view of my days here:
the tops of the hospitals and the city behind,
and it seemed like we were
all in this
together.
It was a most beautiful day, and
I was feeling like a cretin
because I was twenty minutes late
for work.

Some mornings
I wake up with a strange taste in my mouth.
I think I grind my teeth while I sleep.

When I saw
the Longwood train slither away,
releasing itself from its hold
like a slippery turd,
I was too far away
to run for it,
and I said
to myself
"fuck you fuck you fuck you fuck you fuck you,"
though the words
never made it far from my throat,
and I knew I really needn't be that angry.
I pulled out my book and read some.
I read after I got on the bus too.
Bukowski
didn't make me
notice I was a cretin, and almost
caused me to forget that I was
crammed beside people who were forced to be
crammed beside me.

I played 'Window Cleaner' last night
at the coffeehouse
and it went well,
as these things go.
They clap and cheer for everyone and everything
at these things.

But that doesn't bother me at all.
When it came time
to clap and cheer for me,
I thought how good
it was to know
that, along with
everyone else who had
half a soul since Memphis,
I was rock and roll,
I could do this, be
a part of it all and
everything, too, that life
was out there,
in here,
that this life was a hard and
beautiful thing,
that I could take this gal, this life, that had been
with me and opposed
to me every step of the road,
marry her, elope with her,
have her children,
argue with her over the telephone,
and be ecstatic.

The air was fresh and wet and full this morning.
I knew it was stupid feeling like a
cretin.
I really didn't feel like working,
anyway.
So before I passed
the bakery on the way to the office,
I went in.
I like them.

They make these great muffins
for a dollar.
I found out I only had twenties in my wallet
and almost kept going.
I went in anyway.
I got some bread too.
The lady only gave me seven bucks change,
so I had to tell her that
I gave her a twenty.
I put three quarters in the tip jar, just because
they make bread
and I like them for that.
It was too tender a morning
for hard feelings
to survive.

Yeah, if you can
find out about England
this week-end,
I'm pretty much ready
for it.

If it doesn't work out,
that's fine,
I'll go somewhere
else. Or stay
here, though
I doubt it.
Not that
it's really that different here
from other places, but it is different
to me.

I don't feel like a cretin as
I'm writing this.
The feeling passed.
All feelings pass.
Maybe that's
the scary part.
Impatience is a virtue
and I get a little more
angelic
every day
I live
this shit.

I showed up
to work
twenty minutes late
and I went upstairs
to eat
my muffin.

The King's Castle

◆

There was once a king who was so poor that, unable to afford a real castle, he and all of his loyal subjects lived in a vast pigsty. Morning, noon, and night, the people of the kingdom could smell and hear nothing but pigs. While the many pigs that lived in the sty with them provided enough food to survive on, the king, without a castle, felt not much like a king at all. So he sent word far and wide that he desired a magnificent castle to be built, as great as any other castle in the world.

In order to lure the finest builders, he promised a huge sum in rubies, money and gold to whoever was chosen to build his castle. The king could not possibly pay such a sum, as he had little rubies, money, gold, or anything else—except for pork—but he was determined to get the finest castle money could buy, and the only way he could accomplish this was to pretend to have more money than he truly did.

One by one, builders of great renown heard news of the king's offer and arrived at the pigsty. The first builder to arrive was a giant of a man. He showed up with a dozen apprentices, and each apprentice carried several boxes filled with builder's tools. The giant builder himself seemed to be almost entirely made up of tools, for he had on his person a hundred boxes crammed with hammers, nails, drills, crowbars, protractors, rulers, and other, more exotic tools, which the king had never seen before and could not recognize. The king gave the huge man a hearty welcome, and invited the builder and all his apprentices into the pigsty.

The second builder to arrive was a tall, thin, very handsome man. Precious jewels hung around his neck and from each ear. He wore a costume laced with diamonds and pearls. Each of his two-dozen apprentices carried armfuls of jewel boxes, and each jewel box contained much gold, silver, and other finery. The king bowed graciously toward the noble builder, and invited all twenty-five men and women inside.

Lastly, the third builder hobbled through the doorway of the pigsty. The third builder had no apprentices with him. He was an ugly, hunchbacked old man, dressed in rags, with a crooked nose and an unkempt beard. He carried no boxes, and was probably the ugliest man the king had ever seen, but, thinking it would do no harm to let him in, the king decreed that he, too, would be welcomed.

That evening, the king held a pork dinner for all his guests, in the largest and least smelly room in the pigsty. After the builders and apprentices lifted their glasses in a toast to the king and his future castle, the king announced that, as soon as dinner ended, he would decide on a builder to construct the castle walls.

As the subjects and apprentices ate their meal, the three builders approached the king, in turn, to tell him what they would do if they were chosen to build the walls.

The first builder said to the king, "Noble king, I will build walls thirty feet thick and five hundred feet high. I will surround these walls with a moat a hundred feet wide, and fill it with water as deep as it is wide. The gates of your wall, king, I will make of solid brass, as thick as a man's height, so that no spear or arrow can possibly pass through. These gates I will delicately balance on their hinges so that, heavy as they are, a single man standing within the castle may open or close them. In short, your majesty, your castle will be totally immune to any attack."

When the king heard all this he was very pleased, but the price the builder asked for was more than he could afford.

The second builder then stood before the king, and said, "Good king, I will build walls out of gold and silver bricks. In between the bricks, I will place great strings of emeralds and diamonds, so that your walls will shimmer in the sun. I will fill your moat with exotic sea monsters, taken from the deepest depths of the ocean. People from miles around will want to see your castle, and you will be the envy of many kingdoms."

This, too, excited the king, but the handsome builder asked for even more money than the giant.

Finally, the third builder approached the king. The old man told the king, "King, I will construct walls that are perfectly camouflaged against the sky. Your enemies will not be able to find the castle, so they cannot destroy it. Even if they did find it, the walls I build will be totally indestructible. No man or beast will be able to tear them down."

This plan pleased the king most of all, and he asked what price the old man wanted.

"Two pigs," said the ugly old man, "and a pot."

The king jumped at the chance to take advantage of the old man's offer, and gave two pigs and a pot to him immediately. The old builder promised the king he would start building the wall the next morning.

Night passed, and all the next day, and the king was very anxious, for the third builder had disappeared and could not be found. The king knew not what to do. He did not want to be unkind to his other two honored guests, however, so he had his subjects prepare another pork dinner for them, along with their apprentices. Just as they were about to start eating, the third builder turned up at the pigsty.

"All finished," he told the king.

The ugly old builder had finished the walls in a single day! The king could not be happier about the good news. He told the builders that, the walls having been completed, it was now time for him to choose which builder would build the towers of the castle.

The giant builder with the many tools was again the first to speak with the king. He said, "I will build a dozen towers for you, king, that are a hundred feet high and as strong as diamond. The fiercest cannons will not be able to knock them down. Inside the tower, I will place arrow slits, boiling oil, and trap doors to keep out all invaders. No one will be able to conquer you, and your towers will stand for centuries."

The builder's promises made the king feel very secure, and he would have agreed to let the first builder commence building immediately, but for the price. It was far too high, and the king could not pay it.

Next, the second builder requested an audience with the king, and then said, "I, king, will build fifty towers for you, and each will be so large and so beautiful that princes three kingdoms away will stare in awe at them. I will grow ivy and rare plants on the outside, and decorate the inside with fine woven carpets and elaborate chandeliers. Stained glass windows will be seen on every wall. Each tower will be designed in a unique and original way, using a different combination of materials, and each will be a different shape. Word will spread of your great towers, and you will soon become known as a noble and great king."

When he heard this, the king was eager to let the second builder make his plans reality, but he did not have the money to do this. So he waited until the third builder spoke.

"Dear king," the ugly old man said, "Why bother with twelve or fifty towers when you can have one tower that can do even better? I will build a tower so tall it has no beginning and no end. You will be able to see all the world from inside this tower. What's more, the tower will be exquisitely designed, so that once an invader enters it, he will not be able to escape with his life."

Thinking the tower almost too incredible to believe, the king asked the builder how much he would have to pay for it.

"I will do this work for you, king," the third builder said, "For two pigs, and a pot."

So the king gave him two more pigs and another pot, and the old man was nowhere to be seen the next morning. The king, curious to discover where the hunchbacked builder was working, sent out his best horsemen find him, but they returned to the pigsty unsuccessful. Just before dinner, the third builder turned up again, alone, and announced that he had finished the tower.

Things were going wonderfully for the king. The tower and walls having already been completed, all that was left to build was the inner keep. As the three builders ate their pork dinner, the king told them he would hear all their proposals for the inside of the castle, when they were ready.

When the meal was finished, the first builder drew near to the king. He said, "King, if you choose me, I will make the most beautiful domes, giant arches, and grandiloquent architecture the world has ever seen. The castle will measure a mile from end to end, with each room intricately carved out of enormous oak trees. Your guests will marvel at all the wondrous sights around them."

But the giant builder's price was greater than all the money the king could ever hope to have.

The second builder told the king, "Your majesty, in the keep I build for you, every hallway, every chamber, every horse stall will be filled with the finest treasures and jewels. My apprentices and I will create beautiful sculpture and frescoes for your castle, and fill the air inside the castle with the choicest fragrances from around the world. The furniture I design will be as soft as clouds, and as brilliant as the sun. Truly, living in your castle will be a great comfort, the likes of which man has never before felt."

This all sounded marvellous to the king's ears, but as usual, the handsome builder demanded more money than the king could pay.

It was then the third builder's turn. The king said to him, "Old man, if you have kept your word, then I greatly look forward to seeing the magnificent tower and walls you have built. If I let you build the inner keep of the castle, what will you do?"

The old builder told the king, "Great king, I have kept my word, and if you choose me, you will want to keep my keep. It will be made out of every material in this world, and will be larger than any other castle yet built. There is not an exotic animal or rare plant, beautiful maiden or delicious food that will not, in time, be revealed within your castle. The rooms will be a maze, impossible to solve, so complicated that those inside the castle will not ever be able to tell when they have left one room and entered another. Simply put, your majesty, there is no-one who would not be your subject, once I construct the keep of your castle."

"This is no small feat, old man," said the king. "It will take you much time and money to accomplish it."

"Not at all, dear king. All I require is a day, two pigs, and a pot," the old man said.

"Amazing! Well, I shall give you your pigs and your pot right now, and tomorrow evening, I shall see my castle."

The king gave him his pay and then went to sleep, and dreamt wondrous dreams about all the towers, walls, moats and keeps he would witness on the following day. The next morning he sent away the first two builders, along with all their apprentices, with kind words of gratitude, and condolences that they were not chosen to build the king's castle. Then the king waited anxiously for the old man to return. Unfortunately, dinnertime came and went and the old man never arrived. The king was so upset he went to bed without having any pork.

The next morning, there was still no sign of the old, hunchbacked builder. The king felt he had been treated unkindly, and he sent out knights to find and capture any man with six pigs and three pots. He secretly hoped that his men would instead find his castle, that the third builder had built everything he had promised, but the king knew it was unlikely that the old ugly scoundrel had built anything at all, so he did not mention this wish to his knights. The king's men searched for weeks, but found nothing, and the king and all his subjects continued to live in their pigsty.

The king was very upset by all this, and spent nearly every night crying into his pork dinner. Until one day, a wizard came to the kingdom.

He rode on an iron chariot pulled by half a dozen splendid war-horses, all clad in armor. The wizard was tall and wise and handsome. The king and all his subjects stopped what they were doing, and went to the door of the pig sty to greet the magician, for they were not used to so illustrious a visitor.

"Why have you come here?" asked the king. "Where are you travelling to?"

"I am travelling to your kingdom, of course," replied the wizard.

The king was perplexed. "Our kingdom? But why would you want to come here? For we have no reason that would entice you to visit here. We are poor, as you can see. We live surrounded by pigs in our humble pig sty."

"I came to see the castle," the wizard simply said.

At this, the king became bitter and resentful with the memory of what had happened. "My good wizard, you may have received word that we were building a castle; indeed, I invited the finest builders in the world here to build it. But we have been tricked, and have no castle."

"On the contrary," said the wizard, "I see a quite magnificent castle!"

The king looked around, bewildered. But nothing had changed—the land still appeared quiet and empty.

'I see no such castle," said the king.

"Can you not?" asked the wizard. "That's a pity. For I see here," he remarked, tapping the air with his knuckles, "four of the most well-camouflaged walls that I have ever seen. Not only are they well-disguised, but even I, with my great skill in wizardry, could not knock them down."

The king was flabbergasted. There really was a castle!

"And this tower," the wizard continued, "I was inside this morning, I have ridden with my horses all day, and I am still inside it this afternoon. If you had only had the good fortune to travel as much as I have, then you would see that your tower stretches across many lands, all things can be seen from it, and no one ever escapes or steals any bounty from it. How wonderful to have a castle that no-one ever takes things from!"

"Why, yes, I suppose," replied the king, at a loss for words.

"And as for this great keep, is there anything of wonder and beauty I have not seen inside it? It is as if I am in a single room, with all the comforts of home and the exoticness of distant lands. While I cannot find my way out of it, for the path is too complex, I am not sure I wish to ever leave."

The king, looked about him, smiled, and then gave a warm laugh. He patted the handsome wizard on the back, and said to him, "If you really do want to stay, we would not wish you to leave. You have shown us our castle, which we thought we had lost, and I am very grateful to you for this. Please have dinner with us tonight, and for as many nights as you care to stay."

The wizard stayed for one dinner, and for dinner they had pork—and deer that they had hunted, and wild berries, corn, fresh soup, and fine breads, and jams, and sauces from fresh vegetables, and many other things from the lands around them. And they all ate until they were full, and then slept.

The next morning, the wizard rode away on his chariot pulled by six war-horses—which looked curiously, from a distance, like pigs and pots. And the king and all his loyal subjects were very happy in their newfound castle.

Teardrop

◆

We are magical,
We come from stars above,
   We flounder, fuck, and frolic,
And leave our mark on love.
   I am just a teardrop,
Flung down from broken sky,
   The earth will feel me kiss it,
And air will watch me fly.
   Sculpt the mountain, fill the sea,
Mark the time I'll never know,
   This teardrop will in sewers flow,
Skysoul's wondrous aching we:
This rain, it's heart-pain from above,
How many leave their mark on love?

The Nothing

◆

What is the stuff of dreams made of?
  Nothing, nothing, nothing more.
Where does the end of the day belong?
  At nothing, nothing, nothing more.
Sweet thoughts of a maiden who,
  No reason needing,
Gives her all, her nothing;
Unsettled by a horseman,
  Approaching unheeding
Of all but his task, to bring all to naught,
  All cast in emptiness,
  All set in black,
  A sleep's untouched soul
  In a night's barren sack.

A Letter From Duane

◆

Hey asshole,

Wassup? You still driving that shitheap? How many times I gotta tell you, get a real ride and stop acting like a putz?

I'm giving you my masterpiece, cleverly titled "Phat Juice", so you can put it in your crappy book you keep whining about—maybe you'll get your dick out of your ass and finish it some time. Make sure you tell people how it was in that episode of Hard Copy—I'm sure they'll remember the one. Don't mention the whole prison thing, though. Most importantly, make sure they know that THIS SHIT IS ABSOLUTELY TRUE—none of your preppy dickhead fiction nonsense.

Give my regards to your hoochie, unless you've fucked another one over, and if so, got her digits for me?

Yours truly,

Duane Porter

P.S. You better put this shit in, or everything about your "special" wiener and Betty Boop is going in *my* collection.

Phat Juice

◆

It was a sunny day and fucking hot when Dracula moved in down the street on Quaker Lane. Came in on a Mustang Shelby GTI, man, fucking Cobra Jet 428 fucking engine, my friend, 427 cubic ass inches of power, just like a Viper only even more powerful shit kicking its ass. Fucking flew into the driveway in a goddamned beautiful red Shelby GTI, Oakleys on, ribbed T-shirt and kick ass sideburns. Guy looked like a motherfucking movie. Out here in the suburb crap, man, out here in West Buttfuck, we had never seen shit like it. Oh fuckin' A, I thought. Here comes trouble.

Of course, back then, I don't know he's Lord of the Dead or nothing—I just figure he's a New Yorker big Asshole boy who took a wrong turn from his fucking crack whores and Yankee stadium. But let me just spout this shit for the record, before you think I'm some stupid fucking Ward Cleaver who can't find his ass with a vibrating dildo: I clock him walking down that driveway, man, under the fold-up basketball all-in-one basket and net that the Greens had put up there before they jetted their asses out west to Starbucks country—I can totally slam on that shit, man, but anyway—I'm surfing this dude's web and shit just ain't downloading, you know? Like something about the way his wallet jangled on his chain, he's walking like a real Reservoir Dogs badass, scary hot shit, man. I just *know* he's got the fucking eyes of a puma behind those Oakleys, this guy ain't no ordinary prick. That's when the horror flick jitters fuck their way up and down my spine. This motherfucker knows what he's about, no doubt. He's got that phat juice in his blood. The incarnation of motherfucking cool. Pure phat juice.

That shit ain't all, man. This brutha's got the tastiest of taste. House and Garage pumping out the walls, 'cept sometimes he's all about the Bach. Yeah, that's right, the dead maestro dickwad. I figured vampires would be into guitar-driven shit, like Slayer, devil bands that scare the crap out of Tipper Gore and the old ladies, but no, he's a bass and keyboards man to the core. Didn't even put the Stones on, though every asswipe knows the Stones play some damn fine vampire tunes. Played those block-rocking techno beats so loud that the neighbors called the pigs, trying to stop the party, but there weren't no party, just main man Drac cranking that shit *up.*

The cops like him—he ain't a local boy but he's got style—so they just hang around for a brewski then screech Dunkin' Donuts and leave him to his beats. Though how he sweet-talks them pigs I'll never know, 'cuz those West Buttfuck fuzz are the most tight-assed headlight violation pricks I ever knew, and I been down South, man, I seen some not right shit all right.

Anyway, none of the other 2.5-'ers know shit about supernatural crap or whatever, so I keep my eye on that punk's ass. Guess he's scoping me, too, 'cuz one day he comes to *mi casa* carrying a case of Beck's. I'm kind of bummed, 'cuz to me, Beck's is kinda tasteless—I know it's strong and shit but it goes down *too* easy, you know, like an Alabama redhead, and life shouldn't be that easy, like beer should have a kick to it, like drinking it is more of an accomplishment, you know? But fuck it, a beer's a beer, this bud's for me and Drac is still the man. He's said the magic fucking password for all I care, any punk that climbs into my treehouse with a six-pack is welcome to be a part of my fucking not-so-secret club.

He's smiling, but not in a real estate kind of way, he's just like, yeah, I'm hot shit, you're hot shit, the world's hot shit, no hassles, right? Not trying to sell you anything, you know? He doesn't *need* shit from me, which I dig straight off. I meet so many needy bastards in my life, they pretend to like you, only they like what you *got*, man, they like your style, and they want some of that, but it don't work that way, man, style don't have no exchange rate, because as soon as they're friends with you and you're going to their fucking church hall fetes and family dinners, as soon as they latch onto you they become this fucking parasite, and that style is gone, my friend, you're just a couch potato asshole, you're a nice guy, and then you're halfway dead, you're a 401K junkie, and then you're watching that game show or cooking that pasta lite meal, and then they wonder how come you ain't the big man on crack anymore, so they fuck off and let you die while they go find someone else's dick to suck.

But Drac, man, he may have been a vampire, but he just sucked blood, that's all. I mean I could dig that.

So we're hanging ten on the porch, downing a few bottles, just like the good ol' boys in some fifties James Dean shit, talking about cyberporn hoochies, virtual babes and all that junk. He figures a cyberchick is more exciting, virtual pussy is the way to go. I'm not so sure, only I ain't had any in a while, so that kinda makes me want the real deal, *capiche*? I hadn't sharpened my pencil in too fucking long. I mean, I get him and all, the glamour, the way a chick looks and what she's got on, it's even better than the real thing, better than all the fucked-up relationship or one-night stand hassles, but not when you've had a dripping hard-on for six months, not when you got an aching wrist and a soaking wet collection of L.L. Bean swimsuit catalogs, I mean you'll take any kind of shit, right, you'll put up with acne and screaming bitches, and you'll be one grateful son of a bitch. But Drac's hoochie coochie, so the bastard can be style and get away with it. It's all about cocky, baby—the benjamins ain't got shit to do with nothing. You got cocky, if you don't give a shit, hoochies'll be overflowing. That's the shitty twist—if you don't want it so bad, you find it cumming on your fucking bell, while an unlucky dipshit like me is unfucked and horny.

I got these wicked licker-stickers inside, they're seriously phat, they got like Batman and Robin on them, all the awesome Saturday cartoons, but they fuck you up real, real good, no joke. So I take two and I definitely will *not* be calling your ass in the morning, I mean this is some heavy shit, man, any more I'd be seeing God and ants would be crawling everywhere, and I think I heard the fucking tree fall in the forest, but Drac has *five* of those mothers. That's some ultra-heavy fucking shit. That's a month's supply for some Indiana kid, and he scores it in a couple of seconds. The guy wasn't right, that's too much shit for any fucker, even the military don't fuck around with that much crap. I mean, I'm not fucking Tylenol, but I know my shit OK, and I know if I downed five of those fucked-up candy canes I'd be stiffer than Rosie O' Donnell's spare dildo. It just plain don't make sense.

But soon it doesn't matter too much to me, 'cuz I hit orbit a few minutes later and Drac is there already, and he starts screwing around with reality and shit. We're doing the standard high school tab trip crap—we move the walls, make time go all slow, just the basic Intro to Acid 101, but then he gets all cool and creepy. The man is an artist, formerly known as Count fucking Dracula. He's having me see shit where shit really ain't meant to go. Like there's this chair, right, and he starts saying, see the hobgoblin, see the hobgoblin, and I'm looking, thinking what the fuck is this dude jerking off about, and I look again, and it's *right there*, no shit. This thing's one mean motherfucker, it's all bright orange with pimping muscles on its arms and legs, and yellow horns on its head, I never seen shit close to it before. He says like it's moving left to right, and holy hot fuck, it *is*, only this time I ain't trying or nothing, not like the usual shit when it's half your brain and half the brain on eggs, this is totally different. Like, I did V.R. this one time and it was way cool, I chased some doofus around this stadium or whatever, and I was getting really into it, but then when the money died and I took the goggles off my face, I was in the fucking arcade again, and there were some eight-year old punks yelling at each other and I found out I had gum on my ass. So like Alice in friggin' Wonderland I knew it had all been a dream and now I was back in Shitsville USA. But this hobgoblin shit is *real*, no goggles, nothing, real like the gum on my ass was real, only way, way cooler.

There ain't no chair there any more, that's shit's for sure. Drac just says something and Hobgoblin does it, right in front of my face. It's—I mean, I don't know if this fucker's he or she or AC or DC but that shit's too scary for me to even *consider*—it's doing pinwheels and Manga-type shit and flying tricks and crap out of Flipper and the Animal Channel and the lambada with itself. It splits into two and three and does all this crazy shit from Alien, only even fucking Lucas's special effects budget couldn't make this shit up. And yeah, I got imagination, sure, but even I'm not this fucked up. Nothing like this crap has ever happened to my sorry ass before.

He tells me the hobgoblin is coming for me, and he's all fake camp-fire spooky voice, so I just laugh that shit off, but then this mother-fuckin' hobgoblin-chair-what-the-fuck-ever type thing *looks* at me. I shit you not, man. Turns in my direction, and just fucking Superglues its eyes on my skull. We're talking red and glowing, but we're sure as shit not talking Cub Scout Halloween costume, I mean the eyes are *hungry*, they're out on the devil's lunch break and I'm a goddamn Hostess Twinkie. I probably crapped my pants right there but I was way too gone to notice.

I try to make sure my cool's still on the a/c, that I don't bug out or nothing. Must See T.V., I keep telling him, Must See T.V., and he kinda smiles a little. Only this time—and I ain't no fucking hippie Krishna freak or one of those won't-shut-the-fuck-up Greyhound Christians, I mean I'm cynical as shit, the only time I ever saw an Unidentified Flying fucking Object was when I did a poopy off the school roof in third grade—this time I'm looking right at the Angel of Fucking Death. His face glows and there's this weird-ass force field around him, like those whacked dark-side-of-the-Force sparks are popping like crazy around his mouth, like Pop Rocks, only they explode on the outside. Everything's lit up all neon and his face is fucking everywhere—even if I shut my eyes, that crap's already burned into my retina. And that's when I know my ass is off the yellow brick road, 'cuz I saw the wizard behind the curtain, only in this particular motherfucking Oz the little old guy is on the outside, and the real nasty thunder and lightning son of a bitch is on the inside, just waiting for a sucker to peek his ass round the wall. And that sucker just so happens to me.

But the weird thing is there's nothing obviously fucked up about *el hombre*—Judge Judy ain't about to admit my fucking evidence, you know? His head ain't popping off, shit don't seem like the Exorcist, and he ain't saying he's gonna to Shredded Wheat my ass and sprinkle sugar on my dead flesh or nothing, all I got to go on is that weird "maybe I shouldn't go in the cemetery on Halloween when I just tripped over three ugly black cats and a motherfucking corpse" kind of feeling. He almost looks kinda peaceful, like a tiger chilling in the zoo, about to kill me but he really doesn't fucking care. But then again tigers use your fucking vocal cords for Hubba Bubba, so maybe that's why they're so chilled all the time. It's like he's not even gonna *try* to kill me, man, he doesn't need to, this guy's so fucking tough he's like the sun, he can burn you up without even fucking thinking about it. His face is pulsing on the back of my fucking brain but he ain't even moving it. He's just look-ing all calm and shit, and I know his phasers are set to friggin' kill but he ain't showing it, I'm getting worried and it makes me mad dizzy and I think I'm gonna hurl. But he's fucking wine man, he's a fucking danger-ous buzz, and I gotta admit I'm kind of into this shit, the danger, not knowing what the fuck's going on, I mean fuck it, it beats the boob tube. Shit is not of this earth, and it's freaking me out like those big-eyed grey aliens but even those big-eyed grey aliens ain't freaked me out that much, which is some shit all right, because when I was a kid I thought I saw a big-eyed alien out my window, only it was just my cousin in some pine trees, so anyway big-eyed aliens are some serious shit but that's *nothing*.

He only smiles like that a second, but I memorize that crap, man, I staple-gun it to my head. He's almost fucking normal now, just talking about football, as if that's got shit to do with anything at the best of times. So I act all hip-to-be-square too, so I don't spill Drac's beans about him being a freak of nature and all. He's laughing so I'm laughing too but I don't hear the shit he's telling me about, and I figure it don't take Colombo to find me guilty as charged of being a paranoid buttmunch. This drug shit ain't exactly taking me to Jamaica so I fuck up my short-term to give me some shit to think about. That always keeps my ass busy when I'm floating in space. The more I think about my short-term, man, the more it goes. I'm like sitting down and I'm all about how did I get here, where was I before I sat on this fucking sofa, but I don't know how, or why, or something. I'm just sitting down.

Then I start looking at the lights, and they're all checkerboard and shit, man, but that shit doesn't freak me out, 'cuz that's just my standard routine when I soak up the heavies. Even the weed does that crud to me. I just stare at the light, all kind of bouncing into each other, and it kinda squares off, right, like light-dark light-dark, I'm sure Mr. Harold the local physics dude could tell you what that shit means, but he doesn't like me since I smashed up his pendulum in the stairwell, even though I tried to explain that that shit was an accident and I made totally sure I didn't hit nobody, but anyhow, moral to the story, I don't know shit about light.

The crap is in my personal swimming pool now and Drac is saying some shit to me but I'm about as clued as fucking Silverstone right now. I'm trying to scope what he's saying, but I'm distracted 'cuz I'm worrying that I don't know how close I am to the walls on either side of me. Which is typical drugs bullshit, because who the fuck cares how close the wall is, the wall ain't gonna be offended by my B.O., so it's not shit I usually think about when my brain's not calling collect from Wyoming, but then I guess I usually just *know* how close I am to the wall, it's like when I'm not totally fucked up off the radar screen, my body takes care of that shit naturally, subconsciously and shit, and that's why I never think about it. And Drac's still talking, I don't know Diddly to say back to him, how do I airlift my ass out of this snafu situation.

Next thing I know I'm patting some other dude's shaved head, like where the fuck did he come from, just shaved his fucking head, I mean I must have said some dumbass shit like crystal ball or Mr. Clean or something which was stupid because I don't know who the fuck he is and he could be Travis Bickle or Chucky or some crap. It's Drac's house or maybe even some bar, and maybe the bald dude's one of my amigos, only I ain't got any amigos no more 'cuz they always fucking go to Jack in the Box on me, man, fuck them, like I ever borrowed shit from cunt-wads. They can't score two pennies to scratch their ass with, if you know what I'm saying. Anyway, whoever that dude is, he ain't there the next time my brain shifts outta neutral, and I'm going upstairs to toke up with the big D.

Drac's room is the fucking bomb, man. He's got purple drapes coming down from everywhere, and shagadelic carpets that spiral with colors and all that, and—get this crap in your bong and toke—the walls are round, *round*, not fucking straight, like you know how much that shit costs man, they gotta get like special builders and permits and shit, man, no good bringing your average retard roofer in on that crap. But that ain't fucking all, folks: Drac's crib has got—I mean I, like, say fucking 3-D posters and you think total cheese, like some fucking Technicolor roller coaster you gotta squint at for two hours to see, only I can never see that shit anyway, you know, if you ask me it's all bullshit, some asshole telling me he sees some fucking roller coaster with double chocolate fudge, so I'd say yeah man, cool, I saw it, even if I didn't see shit.

But I *see* this shit man, ain't no half-assed Technicolor monochrome bullshit neither. It's dancing devils and big strange eyes and twirling ballerinas with skull faces, I mean Chili Peppers ain't got shit to this. And you don't need to fucking squint, none of that junk, pinky fucking swear, all this shit is *there*. Right in front of your fucking eyes. Six fucking little dancing devils are doing a circle round my brain, and I'm trying to follow all the fuckers but I can't, they're doing fucking John Madden formations on speed, and one creeps up behind my ass and almost fucking slaps me upside the head with the goddamn jester's staff he's got, and I try to head butt the shitty runt, but just when I get close, the devil-dancer turns into a fucking orange belly. And I'm sure that gut is connected to the ass-bone of one particularly orange motherfucker, and I don't wanna look up, but there ain't shit I can do about crap, so I do. And, fuck me backwards, wouldn't you know it's the exact same fucking hobgoblin.

No shit. It sure ain't the fucking Spiderman Hobgoblin jerk-off 'cuz that dude's just a fucking orange skater pumpkinhead punk. This ain't no Halloween trick-or-treater, this is Dungeons & Dragons with a fucking vengeance. Its face is curved all funny like Tron, and it's got these totally blue eyes—not pupils and shit, all blue and clear like fucked-up stray cats. It's got this round orange potbelly and it's kinda short and hunched over so it almost looks like the Indian guy at CVS, 'cept you can tell Hobgoblin can fucking fly at you leopard-style and twist your neck until it snaps, and the Indian guy at CVS can't do that, well as far as I know, anyway, who knows shit for sure, right? And then there's those fucking yellow horns, and they're wriggling around the freak's head like maggots, and then my eye's catch Goblin's mouth and I almost heave. It's got that Drac smile, man, only we are fucking *far* from Kansas, Toto. Shit was baked enough when Hobgoblin was just a half-chair freak, but then I was just *looking* at him, his ass was just a picture, see, but now he's this *thing*, he can waste my ass and he's probably gonna. Fucking Goblin's mouth is all calm and shit but at the same time it's twitching, like it can't stop fucking laughing. I'm worried that some whacked tequila worm's gonna come out of its crazy-ass mouth. That's when I start to get angry, man, it's strange. I never thought I'd be Steven fuck-ing Segal, I always had my ass down for the loser who got killed in the opening credits, but I get motherfucking *enraged*. I may be in a bad episode of the X-Files but I ain't about to take shit and eat it too. I am getting my balls busted by a fucking satanic orange midget and the new guy in my own crappy 'burb. Fuck that. Consider me a fucking Surge commercial from now on. Goblin and Drac are doing some goddamn butt-painful fucking, and I am nobody's goofy fucking whore.

We keep mowing the grass and I'm trying to laugh and play all that Mary Jane hippy shit so he doesn't cotton on how I've juiced that Goblin's in da house. It's all so fucked up—I'm trying to be cool like the fucking Golden Grahams boy, when I know he might banish me to the lower regions of friggin' Hell if I don't look as happy as a Brady. I'm still pissed off but this emotion crap ain't jumping my battery any more, it's actually weighing my ass down, my own feelings have got me in a fuck-ing Vulcan crotch hold, which I guess is OK 'cuz it keeps me from doing majorly stupid shit like punching the Evil Prince of Darkness in the face. Wacky backy calms me down most times but right now I'm just so goddamn *heavy*, like when is this fucking *weight* gonna come off me so I can *move* and go the fuck *home*. I feel like a crappy fly and it sure ain't Charlotte's fucking web I'm stuck in.

We start playing air hockey, which is kinda weird 'cuz I can't figure Count Drac playing air hockey. And the funny shit is he's bad at it too. I think maybe he's fucking with me, like when my Dad used to let me win and shit, I mean it's Drac's fucking table, right? He wants to see how good I can get at this donkey turd, but I don't know how good he is, he's got an ace up his ass or something, like he ain't sharing his Trix with silly rabbits like me. So that makes me *more* pissed, but at the same time I'm kind of getting into the rhythm of the game and shit, watching that puck go plink, plink, plink is some superfly hypnosis, and it's hard to stay angry when all you're doing is playing air hockey. I just keep hoping I don't lose it and fall asleep, 'cuz if I start snoring now the Sandman that is gonna come enter me would be Neil Gaiman's worst nightmare. Drac's talking about Saturday morning cartoons or some shit and I just can't keep the flow, man, I mean this is serious, life and motherfucking death, ain't no goddamn cartoon, how am I supposed to talk about Rug fucking Rats? On the wall behind Drac the orange belly goblin is in my face, it's dancing in 3-D, and I start thinking Goblin's gonna eat me, like it wants me to become all 3-D too but I ain't gonna inhale none of that crazy dope. Once I'm in 3-D I'm gone, man, I'm fucking past the Twilight Zone into the Far Side.

So of course I'm way spooked, but I don't say shit because I don't want Drac to know that I know the score or he'll probably bodycheck my intestines against the nearest wall. I'm getting a serious case of the Noid and I'm trying not to lose it, you know, how fear is good for you sometimes when it keeps you from acting like a dumbass, but I'm so far gone I bet there's steam coming out of my ass. If Drac starts saying Velcome or any shit like that I'm going to fucking combust and it ain't gonna be even close to pretty. I'm just trying not to look at Drac's face, man, 'cuz I'm sure that just looking at that weird shit he does can cause some major nuclear meltdown in my brain, and I ain't taking any chances.

He tells me he's gotta take a piss, like excuse him and all that shit, and I always look at people when they're talking, 'cuz I try to be respectful and shit and my aunt Smelly Vera told me that was polite, though I never looked at her, 'cuz that would immediately make my dick shrivel, no offense to the old douche bag, so I look at him. Which is royally fucking stupid, 'cuz his face is all checkerboard, it's divided into all these tiny rotating Dracs, it's going all Scooby Doo in front of me. All I see is his face, grinning at me, over and over and over again, wherever I look, all over the fucking room, and I'm getting hot under the goddamn collar and feeling like a mosquito just before the microwave gets turned on. A thousand tiny motherfucking Dracs, all spinning and melting and twisting and bumping into each other, this shit is too much for me, and I'm thinking of running to Mr. Harold's for an explanation, fuck his fucking cheap-ass pendulum, when Drac goes for his piss and I'm like, I'm safe.

'Cuz he's leaving the room now, going into the bathroom and shit, though why beats me, 'cuz obviously vamps don't piss and shit, I mean if they did they would piss blood, and that would totally suck, I mean we ain't talking tampons here, so I hope to fuck they don't. But just when I think I'm coasting, the final lingering turd that I got to deal with is, his fucking face is *still there*. Thousands of the fuckers, kaleidoscoping in the light. The main man is still doing his thing in the bathroom, so it ain't no fucking trick of the light shit. I'd run but there ain't no point hauling ass, 'cuz I'm dead soon, I am so fucking dead soon.

Finally I freak. I'm thinking how my stomach is gonna grab my balls if I'm still around to see Drac head out of the shitter, and how anywhere else sounds like a great fucking vacation destination right now. I don't even got anywhere in mind, except if you count any place that ain't this crappy overfucked hellhole. I mumble something about needing to puke or piss or crash or something, though I don't fucking know why, since Drac's in the bathroom and the only thing that can hear me is those faces or that Goblin dude, and I don't think that thing is the type to make fucking conversation. It's hard to walk and breathe at the same time, I almost wipe out and roll down the fucking stairs, but somehow I figure out the doorknob and push my ass through the door—I've never done it that fast fucked up before, a doorknob's like a fucking SAT test when there's that much dope involved—and I take two steps and feel the sweet-ass wet dirt soak into my butt. I feel so heavy but it is way fucking nice to be horizontal. My cheek's pressed against the smooth, juicy grass and I feel great and tired but I'm scared at the same time, like I'm fucking hang gliding without a kite or some shit. But my heavy ass loves being on that ground, it's like I'm sleeping in my bed and that grass feels as smooth as a hoochie's pussy. It's good being natural and shit and I know I sound like a fucking hippy but fuck that, both Woodstocks were a load of shit, if you wanna see people get fucked in the mud go to a strip club like any normal fucker, but hey, right now call me granola 'cuz I'd kiss the motherfucking earth if I could move my face a single fucking inch.

Next thing I know I'm outside this scary old building, looks like a fucking church—when I was way younger, me and another little shithead used to sneak inside the Christpads at night and it was really fucking freaky in there, all fucked-up religious pictures in stained glass and shit, that you wouldn't be able to see 'cuz it was too dark, so you'd go closer, and then you'd go closer and you'd be like, jeez, and you kinda wished you hadn't looked 'cuz it's some guy with nails through his ass or whatever. Anyway I'm not sure it is a church I'm next to, it could have been just some old building with bricks and shit. And the really weird shit is that somehow I know there's a fucking Taco Bell on the inside. Don't ask me how I know, but I can see it in my mind, like I'm some fucking Professor Magneto or something, that if I go inside it'll be all colored up like a fast food joint, and I know that dude Biscuit Boy, his face full of zits 'cuz he's always got a face full of zits, that boy's gonna put Clearasil out of business, will be serving Mexican pizzas and chicken super tacos. But I don't follow my mind, man, I keep walking alongside this church thing, even though there's nachos inside and my ass goes crazy for nachos. Maybe it's 'cuz I never got no money and I've always been too much of a pussy to become some friggin' white trash armed robber. Then there's clouds swirling every fucking way, the wind's so strong it's pushing the fucking clouds around and the air is busting into my eyeballs and hurting my eyes. And I hear this screaming way in the fucking distance, and it sounds like some phat Britney I know, so I'm trying to go check it. And I'm all like MacGyver on a mission, creeping up to the church and enjoying this reconnaissance shit. But then all of a sudden shit goes seriously wrong, and fuck knows why. The screaming sounds exactly the same, but now it makes me feel freaked to the cock-bone, it's like hitting me on a totally different frequency, you know? And it ain't a game no more and my brain is having a mega-cow.

So I keep walking towards this goddamn awful noise and then I see what is officially the world's most fucked-up shit. It's this body strung up against this wooden fence, and everything is just all *wrong*. There's fence posts through its skin, and these mega-huge needles are going through it and sticking out of its neck and eyes, and its skin is all yellow like it's got some disease. Weird limbs come out where limbs are not fucking meant to go, and there are these huge bumpy purple blotches with hairs on them all over, I don't know what the fuck they're supposed to be, and if I go the rest of what's left of my miserable fucking life not knowing, I still ain't dragging my ass into correspondence school to learn that shit.

I get the feeling that this thing wants me to help it, and I know there ain't shit that can be done, but I feel I gotta go be Big Momma Theresa anyway. So I walk along—I got bare feet on and the grass is all fucking squelchy, so I'm thinking how my feet are gonna get dirty and I'm going to have to take another fucking shower, and even though me and show-ers are pretty chill I only like showering in the morning, 'cuz otherwise some neighborhood pervert might look through the window and think I'm jerking off in the shower and be all judgmental and shit and I hate that. Although sometimes I am, I guess, so I suppose the fucking per-verts have got a point. So anyway I get near but I can't see the freak's face—it's not looking the other way or anything but I just can't see its face for some reason, it's like shit ain't focusing. And I know I don't really want to check this shit out, 'cuz it's still screaming and I got the feeling that whatever I see will be smacked to the max with the ugly stick. But then my eyes come into focus and my heart totally pisses over my intestines, because it's the motherfucking Drac that screaming. I thought I got away from that asswipe, he's the last fucker I want to see. Drac ain't no damsel in distress—that shit was all a trick, and I fell for it, gullible dickwad that I am. Drac's mouth opens, and he's got those teeth. Fangs. Fuck.

That's when I first clicked that Drac is Drac, the original gangster of the land of the totally fucking evil. His teeth don't look like much, I know, but if Drac had an AK-47 I wouldn't be scared at all, man, while those little fucking razors have got me tripping all over the panic button. Oh seriously fuck, I'm thinking, but at the same time I figure out how I'm in a dream. And I relax a little 'cuz bad things never happen to me in bed, nightmares don't even count, I've dreamt of witches and werewolf lawyers and the worst nightmare I ever had was being chased by a parakeet, and it wasn't a giant parakeet either, it was a *normal-sized* parakeet, for some dumb reason, so there's no point pissing your pants over nightmares 'cuz they're all so zonked. Now I know it's Dreamland, it's like I'm watching myself on TV, I mean I'm still going through the same shit but it ain't quite me anymore, you know? And I concentrate on the soggy ground my butt is on, ass cheeks wet, and my real cheeks too, but no screaming or knives, just my heart beating fast like jungle trip-hop and my mind losing its shit. Suddenly crap is quiet and I'm all relaxed, like I'm smoking ganja with Regis, and I feel so *fucking* good, it's like I've just cum it's so good, matter of fact my sweat's so sticky it feels like my dick's everywhere and I've cum all over. My white ass is walking up out of the Underground motherfucking Railroad. I'm about to open my eyes when I can *feel*—and this is another fucking thing my body can do and I don't know how, ask an A.P. Bio nerd—I can feel something *running motherfucking at me*. Every step he takes is screw-banged into my skull, and my heart is popping out of my chest Tom and Jerry style, and it's worse than the dream and the nails and even the fucking screaming, it's the worst goddamn thing I've ever felt, just this running, running, running, right at me, and I open my eyes and sit the fuck up.

I can't see shit but I know something's there. It's completely fucking dark, like it looks like there's a streetlight on somewhere way behind me or maybe my skull's on fire, either way it's pretty close to Metallica black. I'm on the ground and Drac is fucking *here* somewhere, you know? Call it the fucking force but I can feel him, and I just know his presence can seriously fuck shit up. It's like I'm on my way to forest moon of Endor and all the fucking Ewoks have gotten crossed with Vader and now I'm gonna face a million ugly robotic rabid cuddly motherfuckers. In other words, shit is bad. If I don't move, I fucking die. So I'm telling myself to get up, stand up, right fucking now, but it just ain't happening, I mean my brain is one of those Nancy Reagan fried eggs, I fucking feel like Nancy Reagan herself right now, probably look like the bitch, and it's not good. I feel like a total penishead but it's just so *hard*, you know, it's just so *easy* to lie there on my fat ass and fall asleep.

Then I hear it—the fucking vampire song, straight from Drac's crib. It's like an unmotherly hour in the morning and he's got the Count Dracula theme tune pumping out. You know the one the freakin' TV plays every time a bloodsucker gets ready to do their evil thang. I feel royally morphined out even more than I feel pissed off, I because yours screwly has finally figured out that the dream was a Freddy

Krueger special, I mean, dream or no fucking dream, it's a part of my life, ain't no commercial break, dude, whatever the fuck it was, Drac and all his posse can come in or out of my dreams as easy as Jason Biggs into warm apple pie. Usually when you're afraid it cuts out at the closing credits, you know, and even if there's a sequel coming up you got plenty of time to veg out. But now I know I'm gonna be scared like this who the fuck knows how long, and my body is gonna keep pumping out adrenaline until I explode, and it's going to go on for *life*, man, no opportunity for fucking parole. Fuck fuck fuck, I'm thinking, and it ain't the Cindy Crawford variety, it's the oh-shit-I'm-gonna-die-right-now word. And I see the light of the door, my house is so fucking close and yet so motherfucking far, and I'm trying to move but my brain is stuck, and I just know that I'm gonna be iced by Drac's five-oh, man, lying there like fucking discount bait.

I try to get something in my body to move, but it's just 404, file not found. And then I notice—it took me a while because my brain is grinding louder than a happy bitch—the music has stopped. It's just fucking silence, it's like outer space out here, like 2001 but without the music, and that's even scarier 'cuz it means that Drac has turned his mood music off and started *hunting*. I'm alone except for somebody who wants me dead, which is just fucking incredible. I bet he's enjoying this shit, man, but I don't think about that mutha 'cuz I'm too busy listening to every tiny fucking sound hoping it's not Drac on the prowl for my ass. I just keep thinking I'm gonna fucking die, I'm gonna fucking die, don't fucking die.

The sun slaps me like a bitch and wakes me up and feels like a massive turd, but it's not that bad, you know, a hangover is never that shit they talk about in health class, like wanting to vomit and the worst feeling in the world, man, that shit was all lies. I mean they fed me that bullshit about time being the only crap that cures a hangover, that's a load of dog's piss, I mean I know they're talking blood-alcohol content, but blood-alcohol content don't mean shit, man, coffee takes away the fucking pain, which is why it beats fucking time, 'cuz it's faster. If you wait for time to work you'll be wasting all morning, and a hangover ain't blood-alcohol content, a hangover's a fucking headache, kill the pain and it ain't no goddamn hangover. All that health class crap was propaganda bullshit and I would've been better off finishing that sweet-ass hole I was drilling into the girls' locker room.

Anyway, I'm lying in my doorway and my door's open and it's morning. Halle-holy-mother-shit-fucking-lujah. Don't know how I got here but everything's as cool as Chester Cheetah. Sure, lying in the front door ain't exactly usual but it ain't like it's never happened before, neither, I mean when I hit the booze and drugs I usually end my night going to ground like a Cruise Missile, only it's more like a Scud 'cuz I never know where my ass is going to end up. As long as the sun is shining and the weather is nice, and the creepy horror music has shut down, this prick is not complaining. All I remember is lying on the grass, don't know how I got from Point A to motherfucking Point B, which is strange I guess, but not in a Twilight Zone kind of way, like I say when a phat spliff knocks me out a lot of times I end up clicking my disco shoes together three times, and the next thing I know Uncle Earl's watching me wake up. Well, I don't have an Uncle Earl, and if he was watching me wake up I'd call the fucking cops, but you know what I mean.

I don't know what the fuck to do so I eat Frosties. It seems a good way to deal with any crazy dope that life tries to fuck me with, just heap some sugar onto those puppies and pop them into your mouth. I like to wait until the Frosties get nice and soggy, people say it's fucked up but it goes better with a hangover and you know, their asses are gonna get soggy anyway, like in your stomach or something, so don't fuck with me on this one, *compadre*. I try and avoid my spoon clinking against the bowl, 'cuz that sound annoys me, and it's weird because I never cared about that shit before my pal Typhoid Duck made me notice how it makes that clink, clink noise when you're finishing up your cereal, and ever since that every fucking clink, clink noise makes my head spin and my fucking teeth grind, and all because of Typhoid Duck. Thanks a lot, you motherfucker.

I guess the next thing to do is make tracks to Angela's house. I say this shit because Angela knows how to explain crazy fucked-up acid-tripped shit like this, but also I go and chill with Angela a lot anyway 'cuz she's my girl. Naw, not like that, I mean I ain't banging her, we just hang out together and she's schwing and all that. People get all fucking When Harry Met Sally when I talk about her, but it ain't like that at all, why does every fucking friendship have to involve bone-jumping. It's not like holing the motherfucking sausage makes you better friends, that crap has been scientifically unverified 'cuz all my past fucks hate me. Yeah, I'm a sex addict when the drugs don't have me by the balls, but

I'm not a total stupid asswipe, I consider friendship better crap then sex in the long run, I mean if I want my hot rod cleaned I'll go find a fucking frat slut somewhere, but friendship is really pretty fly, you know?

Plus, she knows her fucking vampires like Magnum knows P.I. I'm surprised she isn't one 'cuz she fucking talks about them all day long. The only shit stain on the whole deal is she's into reading books and shit, like Anne Rice and all that crap, and for me that ain't vampires, man, I mean who the fuck thinks bloodsuckers are into reading, those Anne Rice-reading trekkies would fucking use all their books for toilet paper if they could really bite into somebody's flesh. I hate fucking books, I mean all those dickheads we read in school like Shakespeare and Janis and Hemingway and shit, except nobody read it because Cliff took fucking notes and we all had to learn how to fucking fuck, anyway. Fucking dealing with condoms is hassle enough, you know, do they really want us to figure out iambic fucking metaphor? I mean what the fuck do they think high school's about? High school's shit but it would be *the* shit if they just taught us about drugs and crap, and not that "don't do drugs or sex or nothing" shtick that old Valium whore crapped out at us in health class. I mean who the fuck is high on Hemingway, Hemingway ain't gonna save your life like a hit of glue did once or twice when I was about to lose my shit and die of boredom and homework and jerking my chain. Words are fucking sleeping pills, man, they're born to be motherfucking mild and I hate them.

So Angela's at the door saying come into my parlor, but she's always saying that Elvira shit and it doesn't scare me no more, though I gotta say it totally scared the shit out of me when I first met her, I mean she wears black and chains, standard goth school uniform, which is just fucking My Little Pony on most high school preppy goth girls, like they're really gonna scare anyone besides their parents with that shit, I mean if I was their parents I *would* be scared 'cuz they're gonna get their ass beat up by some jock, but on her it really did freak me out 'cuz I never fucking *noticed* she was wearing black and chains, since her personality was fucking color-coded with it, man, she's just a naturally dark and scary wicca freak inside and out. She's so fucking confident about what she is, your mind don't even question them fucking apples. Even when she puts that white shit on her face it still works. That chick was born to be dead.

Angela has some fucking Inagoddadavida crap on the old elp but I don't say shit to her 'cuz I need her help, or at least for her to know what the fuck is up when my ass is drained and two fucking puncture marks are in my motherfucking skull. At least then she can tell Mulder the 411 so they can bust Drac's ass. So I tell Angela about last night's journey up shit creek, and she's all excited 'cuz it's like vampires, undead, dream crap, total astrology bullshit, she's acting like a crack ho stumbling into Columbia. I can see she's getting *way* too into this, like she thinks it's fucking cool, and this is not cool, man, this is too big to be cool, like cool shit has gotta be small, like a cool hat or a cool dime bag, a deadly motherfucking vampire is beyond the realm of cool, you know? But Angela don't worry her ass about much, which is kinda dope since it calms me down, just being around the mellow vibes, even when I think they're truly fucked-up mellow vibes. Sometimes I freak out too much, I mean if shit weighs heavy on your brain you don't live too good.

Angela's being a total crazy-ass motherfucker 'cuz she wants to go straight to Drac's to investigate. She wants to see crap for herself, which is fucking stupidness incarnate, I mean it's like I jumped off a cliff and now she wants to join the dumbass cliff diving party. That idea's fucking Polish, there's no way in fuck I'm going back to that hellhole to snuggle up with Doctor freaking Death. I don't know if I'm even gonna head back to mine tonight, what if Drac decides to make a house call, you know? I'm fucking on the Undead's Most Wanted, I gotta get El Vamp out of my hair and off my ass. All I wanna know is how to not be dead, in several easy monthly installments if at all possible. She says she won't waste Drac's ass for me just yet, but she will help me look into the whole fucking heavy freak-killing weaponry situation. Angela's got her shit down on this one, so she's gives me my fucking options, should I choose to fucking accept them.

Holy water's shit because what the fuck's holy, man, vampires don't go to church or nothing, right? And besides, how's a fucking vampire supposed to know that shit is holy, ain't no nutritional information on it, so there's no way I'm going against the fucking Lord of the Dead with a glass of water.

Garlic is the same fucking deal, I mean a vampire's no hoochie, man, ain't gonna be scared off by bad breath. Plus my friend Fred Fred Shithead has this asshole cousin who tried to kill a vamp with garlic capsules, only they don't smell like garlic, right, says so right on the fucking box, and I guess Fred Fred Shithead's asshole cousin ain't been seen by jack shit in a lonely, lonely, lonely, *lonely* long time, man, who knows what the fuck's happened to him.

But a stake, man, I'm down with that shit. Drive that shit in and you got one dead motherfucker, immortal or not fucking immortal. I took another hit off Angela's shit and stood up to get a kitchen knife, but Angela fucking grabs my arm and stops me. She's all no, that wouldn't reach the heart to kill shit, it wasn't big enough, leave that crap for the vegetables. So me and Angela—like or Angela and I and shit or whatever—went to go find something to kill Drac and protect our asses from any spooky shit.

But we ain't gonna find crap at her house. Her Mom is one of those freaks who collect velvet Elvises and all that bullshit, her house is like total white trash. He may be the fucking king and all but Elvis don't have shit to do with vampires. Her Mom's all right 'cept she fucked herself up on Valium a long time ago, I mean I like her and all, but she's straight out of Night of the Living Dead II, only probably a lot harder to kill, not that I'd try to kill her or nothing, it's just that she scares me with the way she kind of always looks like she's watching the tube, even when she's talking to your face.

So we head to my humble but there ain't jack there. Angela figures we'll find some shit in the garage, since she ain't got a garage she thinks all of them are loaded up like fucking Columbine, but that ain't fucking true at all. I mean, my Dad's got a rifle and all but I don't think that'll kill crap when it comes to the dead, I mean they already got their ass shot off or Texas chainsawed or whatever, that's why they're undead and shit, and a rifle ain't gonna re-deadify the motherfucker.

My garage is empty like an unpaid whore, it's all cobwebs and shovels and crap. We're making a lot of noise fucking around in that dump, and I'm getting kinda worried 'cuz Drac's house is just like pissing distance away. And we're fucking trapped in that garage, man, it's like we're on the pot and ready for the Hamburger Helper. If Drac comes in the door I'm a blood Slurpee, I mean I'm the fucking human flavor of the month, man, and Angela too, we're both totally fucking sucked.

So I wanna ditch but I'm trying to play it chilled, I tell Angela we should get some fresh air but she ain't toking on any of my shit. She just laughs, 'cuz she knows where I'm at and thinks I'm a real fucking McFly but I don't give a crap about that, it's way too late to be all Macho Comacho. It's always the fucking macho Tony Danza assholes that get the crap beaten out of them 'cuz everybody knows they're the ones to look for when you want some knuckle-trading, and I'm hip to be a loser whiteboy because it means the sucker punch dickweeds don't even look at my puny-ass muscles. I'm half out the door when Angela gives me her damsel in distress shtick, flashes her eyelashes and all that crap, starts talking like some fucking Southern Belle and says I'm leaving her to mess with Dracula on her own, which we both know is bullshit 'cuz Angela can play hardass with any fucking vampire better than I can, I mean women's lib and all that shit, and anyway even if she couldn't she'd fucking love to be eaten out by one of those undead freaks. She's just busting my balls, and I'm thinking should I stay or should I go and I ain't no fucking Sid Vicious but I stay, because two asses are better than one, or that's the kind of crap that teachers are always fucking telling me, anyway.

I still think Angela's kind of a bitchhole for making me stay here but she doesn't give a rat's pecker. She's hunting through all the fucking wiffle bats and McDonald's sand shovels and old Pogo balls and all that dumbass junk, and then she hits the motherfucking Treasure Island, Shit Central. It's my Dad's old tool box, except he was always too drunk to use that shit, must have been even more trashed than normal sometime and got it confused with a six pack. Angela pulls out this fucking electric drill. This thing's got damage written all over it. My pop's got a sixteen inch drill piece, and I ain't talking about his cock, though I wouldn't know, because my family ain't into that Kentucky shit. But anyway this drill piece is 16 inches by 1/8 inch of solid metal loving, battery-motherfucking-powered. Any undead fuck is gonna feel this thing, man, this mother can handle any amount of fucking evil.

It's so nice to have in my hands, man, it's so fucking *real*. Like I had this broom I used to keep under my bed so I could scare off the bogeyman, and it was such a sweet feeling knowing any fucking bogeyman comes my way I only got to whack it between the eyes, only now I know that shit wouldn't work against no real bogeyman, not unless it was a totally lame-ass bogeyman, but then again, no bogeyman ever tried to fuck with me, so go figure. It just felt so good to have something I could *fight* with, I mean it kinda didn't matter so much if the bogeyman got to me and killed my ass, at least he'd know I wasn't some stupid chump kid who didn't even have a broom under his bed to fight bogeymen with, I mean, I'd get some respect. But no bogeyman's gonna come close to this shit in my hands, sixteen inches of total power, this'd fuck up the Loch Ness monster, damn straight.

But I ain't really sure, 'cuz it's only an eight of an inch skinny, what if the fucking thing breaks? It ain't designed to go through human skin, I mean they have infomercials about this shit, and you don't see nobody bleeding to death. I bet there ain't even anything on the label about it going through seven layers of flesh or whatever, nobody's even properly thought about this junk. And Angela's not making my spoonful of shit go down any easier 'cuz she's telling me it's gotta go all the way through the heart, I mean they don't explode on impact or nothing, gotta fucking chop suey the fucking thing to finish off a vampire. And who knows how strong a vampire heart is, man, could be fucking Teflon beating under there. But we score the drill and go back to Angela's basement, right, which is totally fucking Tales from the Crypt, I'm sure that cheesy skeleton dude is around here somewhere. Scary shit is this is where Angela sleeps—that would scare the living turd out of me. And the *really* weird shit is that there's a multi-colored disco ball hanging above everything, I mean how the fuck does that fit in with Goth? But Angela says it's the darkness that lets the color shine through, though I know that's just her Poetry 101 shit talking.

We're lying on her black rug, and I have no idea where the fuck you can buy a black rug, maybe she just spilled a piss-load of Coke on it or something, but anyway she's got one, and we're figuring out how to kill Drac, 'cept Angela says she doesn't want to kill the dude until she's sure his ass is the Count. So, OK, I understand her being fucking Scully on the whole deal, except my shit is dangerously close to being fried any day now, and if we wait until Drac turns into a fucking bat we might as well fill in the Organ Donor card now. But there's no point fucking arguing with Angela, chick always beats me at staring contests, so I don't bother. She wants to meet the demonmeister herself to get a second opinion, but Drac ain't exactly the kind of guy you introduce your friends to, you know, how do you do, Mr. Dracula, may I introduce you to Angela, and hey, Angela, this is a mutant satanic undead fucking motherfucker. No, I am *not* walking into Castle Greyskull without god-damn electronic machine gun laser beams backing me up, no matter what my friend Sherlock here is fucking sniffing.

So Angela's talking to me about how the Prom's Saturday, so I say, what the fuck, you need a date? 'Cuz we're always laughing about the crappy prom, I mean everyone in the whole fucking school is thinking about clothes and shit, and that's all they fucking think about anyway, except now it's even stupider to think that fashion crap, because they all wear the *exact same clothes*, girls in those big ugly dresses, guys in the ugly-ass penguin suit, it's not like anyone's gonna turn up in cut-offs and a Megadeth T-shirt, though maybe they should 'cuz then they wouldn't look so fucking conformist. Going to the Prom's like enlisting in the fucking Marines, you turn up laughing 'cuz every dickwad looks exactly the same, until you bump into a mirror and see you're the same fucking asshole as the rest of them. Anyway, me and Angie and every other non-lobotomized fucker in that motherfucking insane asylum ain't going. I mean, spend a fucking C-note to shuffle around in a dorky circle to Wonderful Tonight or Lady in Red and then drink some unspiked fruit punch? Thanks, but I guess I'll shoot heroin into my eyeball instead, probably more fun than that shit.

So I tell her if she wants a piece of my man-meat she's just gotta ask, ain't no need for us to go to the gym and dance with asshole jocks and stupid cheerleader sluts. As fucking usual, I ain't on her wavelength, so she has to spell crap out for me. The deal is, since I'm fucking poor as trailer trash and I don't even have my own ride, which is sad as hell 'cuz everyone else scored wheels from their dumb rich parents straight out of nursery school, and I'm a little too old to look cool doing fucking wheelies on my BMX, so the plan is I ask to borrow Drac's car, and then we can maybe scope the place while the scariest mofo in Hell gives me his keys and maybe invites us in for a hell-fire latte. Yeah, borrow the fucking Lord of the Dead, the Big Bad Wolf, the Sith Lord, the motherfucking King of all Hideousness's automobile. I want to tell her to go suck a dead horse, but then, all in one crazy fast second, I think, well, man, this is *it*. This is the moment where your life goes one way or the fucking other, where you gotta choose between enrolling in the motherfucking nunnery or taking your shit out on the street, I mean taking a nibble on the cherry or gnawing down the whole bush, you know? And

I think if you act too smart and careful and all that shit, one day you just become fucking boring, its like you just forget you're gonna die sometime, you forget that you're *supposed* to smoke crack and chase women and get fucked up and bungee jump off the fucking Eiffel Tower, man, that's what life is *for*. Until finally your ass is 95, you're locked away with the other old fogeys, and you're *still* being careful, you're wearing false teeth with extra protein or whatever, keeping your ancient ass alive so you can buy more Play Four tickets so you can win millions to buy more pills and keep you ass alive for even longer, and that's how shit goes for the rest of your boring fucking days. The scary shit is I know I could *be* that old guy, man, I get scared sometimes and I know I'm dangerously close to being all safe and crap, and I don't want to go there. I definitely wanna get old before I croak and all, but I don't wanna end up like a fucking Monkee, man, just a washed up casino circuit fuck who's scared to live anymore.

I tell her, let's do this shit. And I'm impressed with the balls I'm carrying, 'cuz I get scared asking my Dad for his shitbucket Pontiac, and here I am about to demand His Most Royal Evil Highness's 428 Cobra Jet GTI. This is like the commercial break before the motherfucking Super Bowl, and I got all my fucking money on the underdog's ass. We don't go right away though, we down some Ramen to get some fuel in us first, I love that Monosodium Glutamate shit, the radiation totally warms your insides. Angela starts talking about Morrissey, and I don't want to hear any fucking dick about bad depressing eighties bands, so I get up and dump my bowl in the sink—I don't even look at the fucking thing, I just chuck it, like a soldier off to war I don't care about shit like whether the bowl breaks, though it doesn't which is lucky I guess, 'cuz I don't want Angela's Mom going zombie on me—and without even saying nothing I'm out the goddamn door and on my way to the fuckin' front. I don't even tell Angela I'm leaving, 'cuz I hate that polite bullshit, so many people waste their lives saying crap that don't mean anything like Toodle-oo and see you crocodile and thank you so much, can I lick your fucking ass, and you spend half your whole life waiting to get out the front door when the real shit's going on outside. Angela's behind me yelling good luck, she doesn't get bent at me for not saying nothing, she knows I get that way where you just have to *do* shit right away.

My blood's rushing, which is really why I do all this crazy shit, man, it's all about fucking with yourself a little, I mean it's just good to do shit that don't quite make sense sometimes. If shit makes sense, well, you're fucked, 'cuz it's more than just survival of the fucking fittest, you know? I mean, if money and jism were all I gave a shit about I could just haul ass at BK's or whatever and marry some stupid ugly bitch and then I'd be all set. When you think about it, it really seems the bomb, you know? You just come home and release the torpedoes into a waiting pussy night after night and then you roll out the big screen TV and watch Howard. That's the motherfucking logical, Vulcan shit to do, right? Only it don't work that way, life gets easy and then you get sick of it, and next thing you know you're on the web hooking up with some 11-year-old Mexican girlie. You're looking for that ultimate glue-sniffing high, but that high lasts like two fucking seconds and then you need something else, and if you keep doing the same crap until it's Kosher you get tired of it. It's never good until it's fucked up, every fucker knows that.

So I'm halfway up Drac's driveway and the motherfucker pops out his door quicker then a cat in a blender, like he sees me coming or some shit, but he's got all his curtains closed and I know he ain't peeking, I mean he's got better shit to do than neighborhood watch the fucking West Buttfuck community, and he didn't hear me, I think, I mean I walk pretty damn quiet, I got Samba soccer shoes and that shit's made for stealth, ain't no clunky-ass Doc Marten's. But somehow Drac's out there on the porch, and he's got a Godzilla-sized joint all rolled up, and I'm taking my first puff and shooting the shit, not mentioning the car straight off, like the man Kenny Rogers says, you don't show the good shit right away. I mean, spout any old crap at first, just lay real low, and then when things are all chill, kinda slip in what you want to say all casual, like the car just kinda randomly came up in your mind, like you could be talking about Pokemon or whatever but you thought about the Shelby first just by accident, and it don't mean nothing, you're just saying it for a fart.

But I don't know poopy about Pokemon or anything else, either, so I run out of stuff to say, and all I can think of is the heavy shit, like Drac's car and Drac not biting my fucking neck and stuff, so instead of shitting my pants I just relax and blow smoke rings for a while. And I almost panic anyway, because Drac's all hush-hush, too, but then I remember that don't mean shit, because Drac's kind of a Silent Bob type of dude, I mean he ain't exactly a bring-up-the-weather dickhead. He's one of those clever fucks who only talks when he thinks of something to say. Only he don't think like we do, man, not like a thought here and a thought there and just bullshit in between, he's like *always* fucking thinking, always getting ready for the next shit he's gonna do—he's a goddamn time bomb, waiting for you to slip under fifty-five, and by the time Keanu Reeves gets his dumb shit together Drac's already got the next crazy spacecake cooking in his mind.

So I'm talking about the prom and trying to act all fly about it, bitching how it's all a load of shit and it's ruled by Gap kids and student government assholes, and who the fuck wants to be prom queen anyway, the only queens I ever heard of were all beheaded and shit, and that's what I think we should do with these fucking uptight prom queen bitches anyway. And I go back to blowing smoke rings, because what the fuck else do I say, and of course Drac ain't talking, 'cuz what the hell is he gonna say about the fucking prom, right? He probably thinks more about Tori Spelling's left butt-cheek than any of that prom crap. So I choked, I didn't mention the fucking car, and no way can I bring up the prom again 'cuz it'll seem too goddamn obvious and Drac'll be downing my blood like Gatorade. Actually, I'm surprised he hasn't hacked into my neck yet, he must have already ate today or something.

I'm taking deep drags and getting lit up quickly, so I don't have to think too much, 'cuz it's all too freakin' fubar and thinking about it ain't cooling my shit down any. And then Drac gets even more quiet than before, even though he hasn't been saying anything, so now he gets like *negative* quiet, he's just like soaking up all the fucking noise. It's like he's breathing on his spliff and all the motherfucking sounds of the world are getting sucked into him so I can't hear nothing. And everything stops all of a sudden, whacked real-life musical chairs, and I don't know if I should sit down or pussy out and run or charge Drac right here or guzzle whatever sleeping pills I got on me. And we get this moment where nothing happens, my heart don't beat, the birds stop their crap, even the nuclear mutant owl in the next block over who always thinks it's night-time, nobody says shit, even the air doesn't fucking move. Then Drac says, you wanna borrow the car. Totally out of the blue, I mean, how the fuck did he know? Swear to fucking God, I hadn't even looked at the fucking car, and it's hard *not* to look at that car, man, it's like a great ass on a hoochie, you know you're not supposed to look, but it just sucks your motherfucking eyes in and you gotta check it out. But I didn't look at that shit, man, 'cuz I didn't want to become flesh sushi, but if I knew Mr. Evil was a fucking telepath I would have looked anyway, 'cuz it don't make that much fucking difference now.

So my heart's going a buck-fifty and that's not good with the pot messing with my blood and shit, so I'm getting really screwed up in the head. I'm trying to remember who the fuck I am, if I get spaced now I'm toast, so I'm repeating my name over and over—just in my head, I hope, but maybe it's going on out loud, and I'm bugging, because I don't know if I'm talking like a sped in front of Drac, but I just can't stop saying name in my head, my brain's like a fucked-up tripping CD player. I got sweat coming out of every hole and I think it must be totally better than this just to be dead, and not have to act like such an asshole because of all this fucking stress I'm going through. That's when Drac hands me this key with these fucking red flames on it, not cheesy Hot

Wheels flames, like beautiful small little fucking jewels right on the side of the fucking key, how phat is that, I don't know what kind of fucking ice we're talking about here but this ain't no blue light special, and it's got a key chain, just for this one key, and best of all it is in *my fucking hand*, though I got no fucking clue why.

The Count's walking down the sidewalk with me and my brain's overheating with trying to figure shit out, I'm in the motherfucking Matrix and I swallowed *both* of Morpheus's pills, man, I think I'm cruising the wrong way down a one-way street. I don't know how I ended up with this key, man, I didn't ask Drac shit, and somehow he still figured out why I was over there bugging him. I look down at the key in my hand and it's so beautiful, and I thought my cock looked good in there but that wasn't shit, and I wish I had another one of these keys to jangle it against 'cuz I love the sound of two keys clinking, it means you got real power, right, unless you're a fucking janitor, but then again I ain't gonna dare scrape this motherfucking key against nothing else, because it is the most beautiful fucking thing I am ever gonna hold, and even Pamela Anderson's tits aren't gonna that.

I start thinking about how sweet that machine's gonna be to drive, 'cuz I was so into the damn key I forgot about the car, even though they're the same fucking thing, I mean that car in the driveway is what makes the key so fine, but just then my ass is interrupted by the engine purring like some sweet-ass kitty. It screeches out of the driveway and I ain't in it, so I'm fucking confused. I look at the key, with its phat red flames, and I look at the car driving off, and I try to get two and two together but that's fucking calculus when I'm this toked. I look up and see blue, it's the sky, and in spite of all the ass-backwards crap going on I'm so happy to see something I know, right, it makes me feel better that everything in this world hasn't gone totally acid, especially since I'm not technically supposed to be tripping.

But fucking Encyclopedia Brown here solves this case, I figure Drac gave me the house key by mistake. And now I'm feeling kinda ballsy, like

I get this rush, I mean we got some serious drugs in our bodies and shit, sometimes those things are even better than the fucking wacky weed or puff powder even, that natural-type shit floods your brain and you lose it, man, I mean you're worse than a fucking toker, my friend. That's why those joggers are always so fucked up, they clog their brains with that shit, and that's what does it. Once the adrenaline and all those enzymes say their shit to you, you got no choice. Like fucking AOL says, goodbye. And I gotta go straight into vampire headquarters, man, 'cuz now's my chance to get inside and learn what the fuck's going on with this mofo, if I got the key, I got's to use it, right? Only problem is if MC Hobgoblin is around I don't want to know about it, and who knows what other Addams family freaks Drac's got on Security. But then I take all the fucking pros and cons to the back of my mind and shoot them, I make my decision and I follow my body to the door, and then I follow my hand as it puts the key straight in the fucking hole.

I'm turning the key and feeling as cool as the motherfucking Fonz 'cuz I'm not acting like a weenie anymore, and I'm getting ready to go SWAT on this asshole, but then the key won't turn all the way, and then just to make crap worse I can't even it out of the door again. I'm shitting myself 'cuz I can feel that there's something *inside* the house that's pulling the key *in*, and if I lose this tug-of-war, and it pulls me in through that fucking keyhole, there's gonna be some huge slimy fuck-knows-what on the other end doing shit I don't even want to imagine to me. I'm breathing a jillion times a second and yanking harder than a jerk-off, I'm almost crying and I ain't usually no pussy, I mean I didn't even cry at Bambi, well not much anyway, but I'm getting so angry at having to die right now in this shithole town that tears are starting up inside of me, and then, *pop*, I'm on the ground with the key in my hand. I got the fucker, I'm still alive. I run out of there like politicians out of a whorehouse, 'cuz hey, you know, I ain't as dumb as you look. While I'm running I come up with Plan motherfrucking B, which is that this ain't the key to his pad, it's a spare *car* key, which means his real key's probably even sweeter, like have pure gold on it or some shit. But this brother keeps on running, I'd go through a fucking brick wall Wile E. Coyote style right now.

I go to Angela's homeslice 'cuz it's a vampire-free fucking zone, I mean it's got a star painted on the floor of her basement, no shit, she's totally fucking Waco all the way. And there's enough candles in that shithole to cook a pig, it gets hot as holy heck down there, she's gotta always make sure she scrapes the wax off the furniture or her Mom gets pissed. I got no idea what any of that Goth shit has to do with any real fucking vampires, maybe they don't like candlelit dinners or something, but Angela's got to do her devil-worshipping, black boots, Anne-Rice-reading, Cure-listening, dream-weaving, astral-planes-projecting, goat-sacrificing, speaking-in-tongues thing, and I ain't gonna be the asshole to stop her, just in case Beelzebub ever decides to stop by some time for evil severed human kidney tea.

Angela's got some Goth version of Kenny G or whatever, like some kind of acoustic devil music pumping. She's asking me to light a candle and meditate about crap, but I don't fucking need a candle for that bull. All this "mystify your mind" shit, nobody needs that crap, I mean your mind's pretty fucking mystical already, it's all just shitheads who are sick of watching TV, so they try to some other gay flava like meditation, or whale-hugging, or shooting fucking steroids and being a jock prick, or ODing on heroin to look all doped out and cool, or whatever. Their mind just drools over any old shit, same way it drools over Charles in Charge or Leave it to Beaver, and so they pretend they're all about what ever shit their fucking guru tells them to be into, but they're not really about it, they're just being a crappy poser. They make a big deal about the shit they do instead of just doing it, they think life is a fucking Sci-Fi convention, just dumb asswipes standing around picking their noses and thinking they got a life 'cuz they can wipe their asses in fucking Klingon.

I lug my ass out of the basement and into Angela's bedroom and tell her I'm gonna jerk my chain, but really I'm just going upstairs to chill on her black rug and get away from all that fucking Kama Sutra reincarnation crap. 'Cuz anyway if I jerked off I'd probably be thinking of Angela, 'cuz she's the last chick I saw, but she's in the next room and she's a friend of mine so I figure that's gotta be some kind of sin or something. I don't usually think of Angela that way but after all she is a hoochie and all, she's probably got tits under all those black clothes, or maybe she just got like a bunch of dried vampire hearts. So to take my mind off all this shit I probably ain't supposed to think, I put some burn marks in Robert Smith. Angela hates it when I do that shit, but fuck it, it's only a poster, and Robert's ugly ass can only look better with a little fire.

Shit's getting boring so I go back to see what Angela's playing at and there's a fucking fire in the middle of the basement. That freaked me out a little, so I'm trying to remember whether I should go for baking soda or water or some other crap in a can, and whether I should be rolling or dropping or stopping or running like fuck, but then I see the flames are right in the middle of the demon star, so it must be another one of Angela's fucking stunts, some more Satan's ball-licking. That dumbass friend of mine is burning up all her best shit, on fucking purpose, and some of it is really sweet shit, man. Like there's a Tool CD, you know, the one everyone's got, but it still kicks a little ass, and now it's way warped and the plastic is smelling like a motherfucker. And there's her Phantom Menace ticket, and OK that shit wasn't actually up to Boba Fett standards, Angela said she was glad she had popcorn 'cuz otherwise the movie would've sucked, though I don't know exactly what the fuck she means a lot of times, and anyway we're talking opening night here, so it's got collector's item tattooed on its ass. And I'm kinda surprised 'cuz she's stuck this sunflower candle in there that she always talks about 'cuz some junkie ex-boyfriend gave it to her, probably stuck it in her fucking snatch or something, she fucking loves it, only the wick's all fucked and it don't work anyway. But I know it's some important shit to her, so it's kinda bizarre to see it up in smoke like fucking Cheech and Chong. Also there's a comb, and I fucking figured she never combed her hair, and there's a piece of fucking green cloth, who knows what the fuck that snotrag's supposed to be all about. There's some socks that she got on an airplane, Virgin Airlines, man, way phat name, I don't know how they got away with that shit, if I ever get to fly I'll be riding a Virgin, fucking beautiful. And there's an asshole bunch of other shit in there, a whole pile of nice crap all burning up, it's fucking Hell's washing machine or something, and Angela's just looking at it like she's in one of her fucking trances.

Then she lands back on earth, she looks at me and she tells me to throw in something that means something to me, which is a load of turd 'cuz I know she thinks I'm gonna dump my product in there, and there's no fucking way that shit's gonna be for real. Because first of all, that shit ain't worth anything to me, man, I ain't one of those pot freaks who worships the shit or anything, I just smoke it. Until it's racing through my brain, it's just a fucking farming crop, if I threw the shit in now it'd just be like throwing in oregano or something. I don't get massive hard-ons about *stuff*, it's the shit it does to me I give fucks about. Also, there's no fucking way I'm letting all that gear burn out like that, what a fucking waste of quality smoke.

So just to bust her balls I throw Drac's key on the pile, I'd like to see her go pyro with that shit, she can fucking explain it to the Boss. But as soon as she gets it into her pretty little friggin' head what key it is, she's yelling at me to pick it up, 'cuz she didn't know I even *had* the fucking key and now I'm about to incinerate the fucker. I mean she should be fucking sucking my cock 'cuz I said I'd get the prom car and I got the fucking prom car, 'nuff said. But instead she's yelling at me to pick my shit out of the fire, but she can get the fucking key and shoveit up her ass, because I'm sacrificing shit just like she told me, right? It's like if people want you to make choices for them they gotta expect some fucked-up shit, but instead they want you to think the same way as their ass, so why did they fucking ask you in the first place? Angela's having a cow, ungrateful bitch, and she's screaming when she runs back downstairs with a spatula, and she don't cook so I'm surprised Angela knows where that shit is, unless it's like Anne Rice's personal cunt spatula or whatever, then she fishes the keys out of the devil's barbeque.

She's all pissed off and smacking me with the spatula, but that's OK 'cuz I know if you want to make people like the real you or whatever, you gotta fuck them off every once in a while, otherwise you're not being honest, and how are they supposed to find out what your shit's really about, right? But she's not converting my file format right now and she's looking like she might cut my head off with that fucking spatula. So decide I'll go along with her psycho mind game, 'cuz if I don't she might not light up with me any more and that would be a fucking crime. I pick up this knife—yeah she's got fucking knives around, and fucking samurai swords too, everything in the eBay catalogue of motherfucking evil, I really hope she ain't the type to end up in the bathtub with a cheesy this-world-bites-dick death note on the counter and her wrists looking like super rare steak—but I grab this fucking ornamental Japanese knife and I cut off some of my hair. It hurts but in the excitement of everything it's just a speed bump, I don't have time to feel the fucker. It probably makes my hair look all uneven and shit but I ain't fucking Vidal Sassoon or nothing. But I kinda like having hair, you can always depend on that shit, like after shitty days the days when the ugliest of ugly dogs shit on my parade, I look in the mirror the next morning, and I still got hair, and it like reminds me that something in this world is not fucked up, though when I start looking like Uncle Fester I'll have to find some other shit that doesn't change, like toenail fungus or fart noises, so anyway I hope Angela appreciates me doing all this crap.

Angela gets all quiet and shit staring at that flame and my hair burning, so I ask her if she's got any Marvin Gaye so we can get it on, but she says to shut the fuck up and think about the future. She's sounding like a fucking Disney parent, there ain't no point thinking much about the future, in fact you know as soon as something enters your mind that it's *not* gonna happen, 'cuz only unexpected shit ever does happen. So I try to think of the worst shit possible so I can make sure it doesn't happen, like Drac chewing my eyeballs while I'm still alive, or Drac putting toothpicks one by one through my wrist 'til I croak. But then I stop thinking about that shit, 'cuz it's so sick I don't even want it happening in my *head*, and I look I my hair burning, man the smell reeks, I wonder if hairdressers get high on this shit, and I just zoom in on my hair and I start thinking about how everything grows, like you think everything don't move around too much and crap stays the same, but it's all changing every fucking second, growing and warping and whatever, it's like when I cleaned my room as a kid and I really fucking wanted it to stay that way, but then the next day it's be all messy, even if I hadn't played in my room that much, and then my Mom's all pissed at me but I'm like, I can't help it, this shit just happens by itself, it's just the way rooms *are*, you know? I'm looking at my black hairs and watching them grow like fucking snakes, they're all wriggling around there and shit. It calms me down to see them wiggle, it like looks all natural kinda, then I start thinking how cool dirt is, too, 'cuz it makes things grow, and wondering if like, dirt is bummed when things grow out of it, and just when my mind's going wild Angela snaps me out of my shitty trance.

She's spouting some crap about how Drac likes me, so he must want me to confront him, which I think is bullshit, man. This ain't Return of the Fucking Jedi, I don't got any fucking Jedi mind tricks, I know because I wasted four fucking hours one day trying to lift a paper clip and fuck-all happened. But that gets me thinking about Luke, no not the pussy Luke, the one in Jedi where he comes to Jabba's palace and he's got his Jedi's badass pajamas on, and screw me, but I start thinking how maybe I can do that kind of shit, I mean if a dickhead like Luke can get his hand chopped off and come back a mean motherfucker, then I'm sure that after all the butt-juice that I've been through, I can go back to

Drac's and get some respect. Angela's banging my ear with some plans or bullshit, but only a total moron worries about details, I mean, like, those dipshits who go on planned-out bus ride old fart vacations, why bother, when you can just parachute your Harley into Ecuador and see what the fuck happens.

So I let Angela think up all that fucking shit, which apparently is that prom night I'm gonna find an excuse to check up on Drac in his crypt, and Angela will hide the drill in her dress, 'cuz she'll be wearing one of those huge Southern Belle dresses that can hide like heavy machinery and shit, and then as soon he tries to suck the blood out of my ass, Angela will pounce on him like a motherfucker and then he'll explode into thin air or crumble into dust and shit or maybe turn into a bloody bat, who knows. But only if Angela agrees he's a vampire, innocent until proven demonic, 'cuz this is America and all that shit, not fucking Mexico, and our founding fathers weren't total jerk-offs so we have to find out that Drac is Drac before we blow his fucking brains out or whatever. So like once she sees the hobgoblin and all that crap, we'll send the big demon cracker back to the underworld. It ain't gonna work but who cares, strong in the Force am I and I can deal with shit going wrong. And I say, like how can I go to the prom with my hair all fucked up and we're laughing, and I'm thinking this is just like Armageddon where they're laughing before the world's ass gets blown off, and how funny life is when it's too whacked to give a shit about. Just like the motherfucking movies, man, wonder who's paying ten bucks to see my shit large on screen and hopefully get some crotch grapping from the slut in the next seat with the ol' hole-in-the-popcorn-bucket trick.

Fucking prom night and I'm all suited up in my tux, except I still got the Sambas, 'cuz it's gotta be the shoes, man, and I have to admit I look pretty fly. I'm doing my Oscar acceptance speech in the mirror and thanking Courtney Love for being such a great bang, I start the Cuba Gooding Jr. shit when I hear Angela getting dropped off. Check her. She's got this dark blue shit on, strapless, way styling, and I gotta say were she not my friend and all I'd have a serious boner just scoping her. Her hair's all done up, which I always kinda dig, 'cuz it means you can kiss a girl's neck real easy when you're making out and shit, and when you do that the hoochies melt a little, the neck is like a seriously horny spot for them, and so then you can start thinking about the sausage option. But that's probably not such good shit to think about right now, 'cuz we got a date with the Drac-man, and he ain't gonna be thinking about the sausage option, neither, he's gonna be thinking about the transfusion option, and that shit comes with a huge fucking warning label.

So I got her a corsage that's a sunflower, 'cuz I know she goes ape shit about sunflowers, and sure enough she goes ape shit. I'm stoked that Mikey likes it, I thought it was fucking braniac when I had the idea, I wasn't even gonna get a corsage because that shit just reeks of fucking preppiness, but then I remember Angela always going on about sunflowers when they're on TV or whatever, so I got one from the field with 18-Foot bulldog, this massive pimping beast that loves to bite the ass off little kids, but he wasn't there when I went to the field so I snagged a free sunflower. I put it on her, man that shit's harder than unhooking bras, and we're looking like a million bucks in a G-string.

We walk our asses over to Count Chocula's, and there's the car, oh my Lord I have to drive that son of a bitch, and my head goes all funny looking at that thing, it is so fucking phat. No sign of Drac, the curtains are all down like always, the place looks fucking dead. I ask Angela if she's got the drill and she taps her dress, the shit's inside. So we're fucking all Buffied out and all we need is to slay our vampire. Where the fuck is that cunt? My senses are up, it's like when I play laser tag and I'm really ready to kill somebody, when it goes way beyond the plastic guns and the points and the cheesy spaceball scenery, and becomes a real 'Nam experience, blood, sweat, and piss, I mean it's fucking Lord of the Flies time here. I'm doing that just-walked-out-of-a-fucking-action-movie walk, you know, the don't-fuck-with-me-walk, when you're just hoping you bump into another don't-fuck-with-me so you can show your stylin' ninja crap off, except I'm not so anal-headed I'm gonna try that shit with Drac or any other members of the Devil's WWF, 'cuz I know they'd do Globetrotter shit with my head. The whole walk's just to get my game on, so I don't pussy out at the first sight of the big-ass baddie.

So Angela's mumbling some shit in my direction about how we have to go in and talk to Drac, I mean I know we got the fucking drill and all, but if Drac ain't home, we'll have to say hello to the fucking hobgoblin, and if that thing answers the door I'm definitely gonna blow chunks. And I *know* something is screwed way past Hell, 'cuz Drac should be out here, dude is always out on the porch before I get there, no way does that brutha need to wait for the fucking doorbell to ring, he must have known we were coming and decided to fuck our minds up with a little hide-and-go-seek. That gets me thinking he might not actually show up at all, which I'm almost kind of hoping for because I'm scared as shit, but at the same time would be majorly crap 'cuz it means we can't kill his fucking underworld butt and, even more shitty, it means he might not be cool with me borrowing the car. This is bad to the motherfucking max and my stomach feels like it's on crack, and reminds me of my Mom taking me to Kindergarten, my guts are telling me that I should be turning around but I'm still walking, walking toward shit I should have nothing to do with. My legs are like strapped to the escalator going to the bottom floor of Hell's Mall, and the worst thing isn't where I'm going but what makes it worse is how *slow* this shit is going, it's fucking torture.

And I finger something in my pocket to score me some confidence, only it ain't my cock this time, it's the fucking key. And one second later my inner snowglobe is all clear, 'cuz I see what I got to do—get in the sweet-ass Shelby. Screw Drac and his fucking house, screw asking his evil permission for anything, I got the key, right? Let's play this shit on my turf, my rules. The next thing I know Chariots of Motherfucking

Fire is playing inside my head and I am running to the car, I mean I am running to *my* fucking Mustang Shelby GTI 428, man, the mothership is calling me home. It's red, it's mine, I am going to pop this car's cherry so hard it'll know its Daddy. Angela's yelling my name but the only words in my personal vocab quiz are car and ride, the skin on my hand touches the door and I merge with the metal, I am king of all Robocops, utterly fucking invincible. I open the door to a Whole New World, where crappy ol' Disney has been buttfucked and yours motherfucking truly is in control. Angela's still staring at me all dumb-assed, but fuck her right now 'cuz I got the power and I need this fucking car, man, I believe I can fly and God is my fucking co-pilot. Ladies and gentlemen, start your fucking engines. I turn the key.

I've never heard a bitch sound this good, never heard any fucking thing sound this good. When the false teeth folks say those were the days this is the crap they were talking about, although they ain't known shit even half this good, this is *my* magic, holy, poontang-fucking moment, right fucking now. I put the clutch down and feel my foot making sweet love with the engine. I slip it into first, ease off the clutch and feel myself cumming into all the heavenly angels. I roll slowly, the asphalt below us, my baby Shelby and me, and I'm just fucking Zen with everything, I don't care about me or Drac or Angela or the trees or the sky or the Brat Pack or fucking Christina Aguilera or all the places I've never been to or absolutely nothing at all, I don't care about any of all that shit, it's like everything in my life is blended together into one fucking jumbo-size strawberry milkshake, and it tastes totally fucking delicious.

Then I pump the motherfucker. The engine revs and we are fucking flying. Faster than spit we're out on Quaker Lane, lucky there ain't no cars, I would totally trash any fucking VW that gets its sorry ass in the way, even a fucking tank Volvo SUV would be a crappy five-cent tin can if it got in the way of my monster machine. This is the fastest I am ever gonna get, and it feels right, man, I just woke up to find out I'm

Superman, my girlfriend's Lois Lane, I got X-Ray vision and I am about to kick some nasty evil butt. All this time I figured life sucked, and now I know the reason was because I was never going fast enough, dude, and now I'm here, I mean, this is *it*.

Next fucking millisecond a loud-ass sound is raping its way into my ear and a telephone pole is up against my leg. I can feel the wood through my fucking jeans. The world sounds so fucking quiet, the car is sizzling, I mean it used to be a real mean growler and now it sounds fucking polite, almost like it's apologizing for losing its shit back there. There's all this smoke going up, and I'm sure the smoke signal this Cobra is sending is I'm fucked and I surrender. I open the door and roll out, slump my shoulder against the road, I fall down quick like when I was a kid and I was really tired, I used to jump on the bed 'cuz I was in a hurry to get to sleep, so I'd just turn myself into a ball and throw myself on top of the sheets, and that's just what I want to do now, man, but instead I get up off the asphalt, and look at the carnage that is my formerly sweet-ass ride. It don't look too schwing anymore, something's missing, like you know how apart from tits and ass it's hard to put your finger on what makes a pretty babe different from an ugly bitch, but you know there's something, well, that something is missing from my friend Shelby, and now it's just a load of steaming scrap metal crap. Telephone pole's right in the middle of the fucking car, passenger side, like it was a fucking special added feature or something. Crash test dummy woulda been a fucking crushed Styrofoam cup sitting there. Shit ain't broken on my bad ass but I'm not sure I can convince my legs to work. My mind's rolling but my body's still in fucking shock. It's like it don't want to cause any more trouble, so it just shuts up.

I got red shit on my palm, it's fucking blood, but it's OK 'cuz I just fell on my hand on the asphalt. That kinda shit doesn't freak me out, I like blood, especially how fast it heals itself, faster than a slut's heart. The shit is still sending pain signals to my brain, but I just ignore it, 'cuz it ain't shit to worry about. I suck the blood so Drac doesn't get his fangs on it. It tastes good—I remember the first time I tasted that shit, when I fucked myself up on the swing set, and it tasted too strong, it's got like a kick to it, you know? But then, same deal as alcohol, I started taking little sips whenever some bully son of a bitch cut me, and pretty soon you get the hang of the fucking kick and it's like Juicy Juice to you.

So I'm the bastard who killed Kenny, and Drac probably has dibs on my soul, so I'm not feeling too good when I head to the house. I can barely move my neck that shit hurts so much right now, I know those whiplash moaners are all suing liars but it turns out that crock of shit is actually true sometimes, turns out bones and muscles don't get on too good with telephone poles, go figure. I'm trying to move my head a little bit, so I look up and Drac's on the porch, and he's *laughing*. His ride's been fucking recycled, and his shit is cracking up. He ain't just chuckling or nothing, this motherfucker has *lost* his *shit*. He's really scaring me, this guy is seriously fucking psycho, I mean, maybe he's an insurance junkie, but this is a fucking Mustang Shelby GTI, man, don't matter about the money, you get pissed when that thing cracks a headlight, and now it's fucking totaled. Insurance makes you fucking pay anyway, like with my friend Supafine Rick when he drove his shit through a Drive Thru window, and his Dad had insurance up the ass but they just jacked up his rates so he got totally screwed even though he was insured, I mean what the fuck is with those bastards? And anyway Rick had a fucking '85 Mazda, and it wasn't a fucking Cobra Jet 428 engine, I know that shit for sure. Some people go all fucking road rage on your ass if you scratch the bumper on their Chevy Chevette, and Drac's just had the world's phattest car turned into tin foil, but he's laughing like he's a fucking front row tourist at Letterman. I don't know, maybe he can just pick up another one from Satan or whatever.

I'm walking over and Drac's got a beer in his hand, and he's telling me to have one. He can't stop his ass from laughing and I'm wondering when he's gonna go Joe Pesci on me and cut my balls off. I'm caught in his fucking tractor beam, I just stop thinking and walk toward him, though I still don't really feel my legs, but they must be working, since I'm still moving. My head's not feeling too good, it's fizzing like a shook-up Sprite bottle and I can't concentrate on nothing. Angela's looking at me and she's as freaked out as I am, I mean when is Drac gonna go spastic, right? And his eyes are wide open, which looks really weird when he laughs, they're fucking huge, and something's not right but I can't put exactly my ass on it. Then I see it—the tiny spinning Drac heads, they're all inside his eyes but then they get bigger and bigger 'til they pop out into the world and then they're fucking everywhere, all around me, spinning in circles and getting bigger and smaller, and worst of all, looking right fucking at me. I can't believe this shit is happening again, I thought that junk had left my brain, and now I've got a million Drac eyes checking out my blood type. My ass is a total goner. And I don't know why I even bothered, man, 'cuz it's not like there was ever shit I could do against Drac. He's just a different *class*, I mean he's like a fucking Honors human being, and vampire thingy, and I'm just a retard, what the fuck have I ever done besides smoke a bowl and watch ER? I'm about to face my death and shit, I'll only do this crap once, and I always hoped I'd at least like get in a gunfight with Charles Manson and get my head blown off with the cameras watching, but this is the way I'm gonna go, all my juice sucked and not even a TV special, and Drac don't even care, like this shit ain't even an HBO event to him, 'cuz he could turn me into a hemo-addict anytime he wants to, and he knows that shit way better than I do.

So I'm looking at those creepy hypno eyes, and not paying attention, plus my whole body ain't saying Polo when I say Marco, so I fucking trip over and land on my ass on the sidewalk. This splits Drac's ass-cheeks even more, like he's watching America's Funniest Home Videos, only that shit ain't funny, so who knows why Drac is laughing now. Even Angela's laughing at that shit, like it's so fucking funny I can't walk, and excuse me, Angela, we got a vampire to destroy here, so shut the fuck up. I always thought she was smart but sometimes she just doesn't understand shit. And I ain't scared no more, I'm fucking raging instead, 'cuz I'm looking at Drac and I hate that undead fuck. He thinks I'm a fucking food product, that there's no way I can fight 'cuz I'm just his bag lunch, and he can laugh at me and I'm just going to suck it up. And I think how *lucky* I am right now, 'cuz I'm angry a lot but never at the right time, you know, like two seconds after some pee-hole has called me an apefucker or whatever, and you've got all this anger but the ass-hole has already driven off or gone home and you're there punching the wall, and a wall never seems to feel enough pain. Well, now I just got hosed by this cunting vampire, and thank fuck, 'cuz now I got the perfect chance to even the score, and trash some evil as well, just for extra credit. And maybe I'm not a fucking cool-ass vampire or whatever, maybe I'm an average dipshit or even worse fucking crap, but I don't care 'cuz I got a fucking energy running through me, I'm not gonna get rammed in the ass with Drac's prick any more, he may be about to kill my ass but he's gonna remember who the fuck I am forever.

Angela comes over to help me up, which is very gentlemanly and shit, even though she is a chick and shouldn't be worried about that whole deal, I can fucking pick my own ass off the floor, and besides I got shit to take care of. I'm up and the world is spinning and Drac's eyes are bigger than the whole fucking world now, and I can hear his laugh in my head, like it's not even coming from over there, and my blood is rushing all over my body and it's taking control. I put my hand in Angela's dress and get the drill, not like I'm a molester or nothing, but I need that drill, I'm not even thinking about any sexual shit, it's just like a coach slapping Latrell Sprewell on the ass, man, it's definitely not a between the sheets thing. And I'm a total distinguished fucking gentleman 'cuz I don't even feel her up while my hand's in there, it don't even cross my mind, which is weird 'cuz, honestly, it ain't often I get too close to some snatch.

It's heavy in my hand, it's fucking pure power and I'm running all the fuck out at Drac with the drill like I'm fucking Chips on a fucking sting.

And Drac sees me coming but he ain't moving, man, he just looks kinda calm. It's some freaky shit, he's just sort of looking at me and not smiling or frowning or yelling or nothing, like he's not gonna lose his cool no matter what. I flip the switch and the motherfucker's on. This shit ain't even laser tag, this is fucking G.I. Joe on steroids. I'm up the steps, one jump, don't even bother stepping on those fuckers. I almost stumble when my Sambas hit ground, but I gain my feet fast as shit. I can smell Drac now, I don't know what he fucking smells like, he doesn't smell like anything, but anyway I smell how close I am to that shithead. Drac puts his hand up, but I ain't in the mood for fucking high fives, I dodge his hand at the last second and smash my drill right through his goddamn chest.

Right the fuck fucking through, no wonder they call that shit power tools. I dig around a little, not really 'cuz I'm trying to or anything, just 'cuz I can't fucking stop because I was running so motherfucking fast. I drop the drill and my hands are fucking shaking, and I quit cigarettes two years ago. The drill crashes against the porch and keeps going, man, you can't stop that shit. For some fucked-up reason I get worried that the drill's gonna go through my shoelace, I mean what the fuck, who cares about a fucking shoelace? But I'm staring at the plastic bit on the end of my lace and at the drill piece still doing its shit, and I can't help thinking about how close they are to each other, and how I gotta keep shit separated. The drill might go through my fucking ankle but I'm scared about my shoelace, like Sambas are pricey but not that fucking pricey.

There's all this fucking blood and shit on Drac. I hadn't had time to listen but I remember he kinda screamed or something but it was really fucking soft, like he wasn't really screaming he was just saying something or whatever. He's standing there, and I know it wasn't a long time but it's all fucking slow motion and shit in my brain, so it seems like forever, then he kinda slumps over the railing, he's just looking at something in the fucking grass, or maybe he ain't looking, there's a ton of blood, and he's all shaky, like he's trying to figure out where the fuck to put his fucking hands. He's just like *there*, he's like the lord of the dead and all but now he's a fucking part of all this shit, part of all this shit that me and Angela and Ricky fucking Martin are a part of for all I fucking know.

And I never did go to that goddamn prom.

Michigan

---◆---

If it were all over—
    Sycamore green, stroked by the motelled outcast of a wind,
      Hammocks, bound in rope, the taut sky fastened to the fragile
waves,
    fastened to the fragile waves,
      fastened to the fragile waves,
If it were—
That I—
    Reneging dust, settling and settling amongst its kin,
    Bunched arthritic branches, their gentle tips outstretched to pacify
each newborn moment,
    Lacerations of liquid compassion upon a duly smooth and polished
rock,
Should this edified life, so hurriedly dammed,
Let transpire its bladdered burden, and yield an elderflower potency,
    As a pregnant, swollen heart stumbles a beaten path through heaven,
If a mislaid guppy is succumbing to an uncovered fate,
If a sucked cherry stone, dry, lies upon the ground,
    Would this man—
      Tympanic sunshine, distemperate oceans—
        Be any the less?

Cat-sitting for Schrödinger

◆

Well the cat, at the moment, is fully alive, and moreover,
not a bit dead:
I know because it's purring contentedly
on my lap, slowly digging its claws into my leg.

Everyone else has not (yet) been so lucky.

Wilbur had his bones crushed by a falling milk truck,
which, I pray, is doing its rounds only in a parallel universe; likewise,
I hope that the Mafia's gunning down of my friend Jane
is not a permanent state of affairs,
and that Kaleigh's bizarre death
from the teeth of rabid beavers
collapses under further observation.

But it's not all doom and gloom out there:
my Portuguese friend Enrique and Anabella from Bali have been wed,
and will remain so, until I discover otherwise; astonishing, really,
since they hadn't been introduced as of last week.
My three hundred pound friend George has been called up
to play for the Red Sox, and part of me

is rooting for that to stay true,
even though many lives would need go amiss, I imagine,
to put George on First.

And, hey, we all won the lottery.
Even those of us who didn't get tickets—we all have
the winning ticket stuck to the sole of our shoe, and haven't
found out about it yet. Or not.

I leave my sole unchecked—the cat
does not much appreciate my shifts in position.
A pain shoots from my leg and arrives at my mind,
as real as real can be.
When I blink, everything happens
to everyone under the sun,
except my painful kitty.

Someday soon, I will see
this friend or that, and everything will be all right,
but only all right, and not perfect,
and only for a time, and not forever.
I like those days.

For the meantime, I draw comfort from the observable,
inescapable life
of this sharp-clawed cat.

Four Mornings

◆

Tuesday, 11:05 a.m.—I wake two hours later than intended. For a moment, I think I will slip into one of the bursts of impotent, self-loathing fury that often accompany these discoveries of new depths to my laziness; but a feeling of acceptance microwaves within me. I was, after all, awake until three—eight hours of sleep is surely permissible. A writer needs his sleep, right?

Today is the day I finish my little one-act drama. When three o'clock was happening I divided the work into specific tasks: a read-through for dialogue, one for blocking, a quick run-through of all thirty existing words in the Balvissian language to achieve consistency of grammar, a spell-check, a cover page, and then printing out two copies of the damn thing, during which I plan to enjoy, as Fry touchingly put it, "a celebratory bout of masturbation". The future is mapped. I try not to think of it as a plan, for these were events that would occur, regardless of my character or deeds. These events had to occur, because the 'otherwise' involved video games, and filthy jobs, and procreating, and participating in our gross democracy, too big for compassion and too small for justice, of acquiring manufactured items, and never losing anything, of leaving my little world, my spiritual writer's yurt with ornaments hanging on the wall and room enough for one or two guests to come and go, well insulated for sound, and walking into the crowded mess hall most people have to deal with every day. So the plan going wrong did not bear thinking about.

I flip the switch, and the computer groans to itself as it wakes. Last night I had promised myself I would never again play Hearts or Minesweeper. I play a quick game of Hearts before I begin. A 'game' is made up of several smaller games, the first person to reach a hundred losing and the lowest score winning. I don't win this time, Ben does, my virtual arch-nemesis, doomed to spend eternity on my right. I hate Ben deeply. The other two, Pauline and Michelle, I don't despise the way I do Ben, who taunts me by throwing bad cards in my path every chance he gets. Pauline and Michelle I have vague erotic feelings about, even though I never visualize them. I just think how I'm going to beat them, stuff it to them—the 'it' in this instance being the Queen of Spades. These are somewhat vicious thoughts but as a writer I'm permitted to entertain these kinds of thoughts, 'getting into characters'. I get into a lot of characters these days.

I still can't write, do what will be done, even though I know it will be easier today, as I don't need to drag and drudge as many grudging lines out of thin air, and only have to review. I head downstairs with my note-book, to the VCR, and go through my Balvissian as I watch *Rushmore*. I compliment myself on a clever arrangement, allowing the movie to inspire and relax me as I get some work done, and thus trick my mind into thinking it's not work. It's hard to believe, lying on the old sofa, tucked up in my blanket with a coffee, that I'm doing something useful. Maybe I'm not.

I go back upstairs and stare at lines of my old words. My procrastina-tion is maddening—all I want to do here is scroll down the page and read; I know that in doing this I'll be compelled to work on the more disgustingly awful lines. Perhaps to avoid this disgust, my hand on the mouse won't move. The clock yells at me from the lower corner. I stare resolutely at the glowing screen in front of me; I can't let the corner of my eye catch the ridiculous gallimaufry of junk that is conquering my room and threatening my sanity. There are papers, clothes, and knick-knacks everywhere. I don't know where half of this stuff comes from, and I have even less idea where it might be headed. It's getting so I have trouble walking from one end of the room to the other. Yet I don't force myself to neaten my surroundings: I figure, if I have the energy to clean a room, I have the energy to write a sentence, I consider the latter to be of greater urgency at any given time. Cleanliness may be next to godliness, but creativity, for all intents and purposes, is the same thing,

My father is due back for lunch soon—time moves in weird ways for me now, I can't control it as well as I could in the nine-to-five. It spurts and halts, runs away from me when I'm not looking, and other people seem to move on an altogether different timescale. I suspect that, contrary to my naive expectation, I now own less time than I used to, and must learn to spend it frugally.

I open a new browser window and write what is, while I'm thinking of it, the greatest poem ever. All poems are, for a time. It's about freedom of speech and is sure to get the quasi-liberal's dander up as 'nigger' is used in the first line. It gets wonderfully worse from there. As I write I hear myself read it, psyching myself up with its immediacy, although I know it'll be weeks before I address a cluster with this thing.

It's over in an hour and a half. Who but a writer gets to orgasm for an hour and a half? My mind ticking along with my body, breath, blood: everything moves, and somehow from this I create. Each pulse builds toward the whole experience; each brainwave recreates the fading pleasure of the one before it. My minds pumps a hundred thousand different pumps in a hundred thousand positions, each wholly in sync. Whole worlds appear out of nowhere. I beg for more, and get it. Just when I think I can go no more, a smidgen more comes from somewhere within me. That's often the best bit.

The inspiration out of the way, I begin reviewing the play. My father is home, says hello, eats lunch, and goes out to play golf. He's on sabbatical now, undergoes a similar rhythm, on different hours. We're going through the same things, alone. I suppose it is a lonely life being a writer, as they say, but you don't think about it much. I see people in the evenings—away from the office, as it were. It was nice going to work with people, but even then I was known for staying in my corner most of the time. I would come out to talk to people—if people approached me they'd find me remote, aloof, until it seemed to register in my brain that I was supposed to be participating in a conversation—this is, in fact, exactly what was happening—and I turned toward them and animated myself. The thing is, I'm a very slow thinker. It often takes me weeks to finish a single thought. So my mind can be a bit reticent about getting out and meeting the neighbors.

The play's done three hours later. I turn the printer and the shower on. I try not to think about it, as I know I'll cringe at its incompleteness, its falsehood, the parts that I abandoned, its lack of genuine ideas. It's not supposed to be good. It's merely supposed to be done. I'm twenty-four, and won't be clever until I'm forty-eight. And Shakespeare started at twenty-six, so I'm ahead of the bastard. He finished just past forty but I'll be late on that score. I don't need to be as good as him, not ever. Just good. As Michelangelo said, looking at the paint dry on the Sistine Chapel, "Fuck it, it'll do." Well, he probably said something like that.

I have written a play: I am king of all the heavens and the earth. I bind it up in trendy report covers and admire my name on the front page, the name led to by my fathers and grandfathers, my mothers, grandmothers and the careless acts of god. If any urge to resume writing loiters I suppress it: not just yet. I'm rational enough to pay attention to the subliminal, and I induce future writing toil by the reward of Hearts, Minesweeper, and reading Shaw. I follow along to Goodfellas with the screenplay and a notebook, making notes like, "The foot shot—spaghetti blood" and 'Clapton montage—speed changes, extend the climax'. I rewind Batts getting beaten four times, acts I imagine must be simultaneously amusing and irritating to my Dad, who is watching baseball on the other side of the room. I have to go pick up Ted and his pals and return the video, so Henry Hill is never caught and ends up on a cocaine high.

Wednesday, 8:12 a.m.—Shareep is shuffling about in the bathroom. He always takes forever in there, how clean can you possibly get? I lie on the sofa a while, wondering how long I can avoid being, in any assertive sense of the word. No trace of a hangover, for which something out there deserves my profuse thanks. I throw the sheet to the floor and get off the couch. I won't bother with a shower or a teeth clean right now, having neither toothbrush nor towel. If you encounter anyone on the way home, I tell myself, keep a distance and don't talk squarely in their direction.

Shareep steps out of the bathroom. I step in, to have a piss and wash my face. I shove a fingertip's worth of toothpaste around the nooks and crannies of my mouth, although I doubt this will make much of a difference. Shareep asks through the door do I want a bagel. At first I don't think I do—my basic urge in the morning is to turn away everything advanced on my person, until I've woken up enough to know what I'm dealing with. But then my precept to never turn away free food supervenes, and after a long series of 'um's and 'ah's, I accept his offer. I've finished my two-minute morning procedure, and though the needs of hygiene hardly seem met, there's not much more I can do, so I exit. Shareep goes back in and gets dressed, comes out to meet the world in his suit and tie. He looks about as professional as Shareep gets, which, thankfully, is not horribly so.

Shareep's studio apartment is composed of a drably carpeted room, large enough to contain a bed and a sofa, adjoined by a compact kitchen and a bathroom. It's kept quite tidy: the only possession Shareep takes much notice of is the big screen TV, which occupies a prominent position across from the couch I spent the night on.

"What an ungodly hour of the morning." I always say this. Usually shortly after waking at noon. "I know. They shouldn't make people work this early," he always replies. I pull open Shareep's silverware drawer, find a solitary teaspoon, and use it to scoop up dollops of cream cheese and smooth them on my bagel. I generally don't think I like the stuff, but as it's on the counter I might as well mix its taste in with the bread. There is something beautiful, in a small way, about all of this—the food, the friend, even down to the way the bagel looks on the plate. I think to myself how it's maybe just the appreciation of these little unexplained happinesses that I'd like to get across in theatre or film, but it takes years to learn how to do that. Simon and I discussed once, how, walking around Prague and London, we'd have these epiphanies about everything being absolutely wonderful—not on any sort of 'solution for world hunger' level, just within vagaries of breath or the glint of a shop window.

We have separate cars, so after I've thrown my plate in the sink, I could just leave, but I hang around and wait for Shareep to finish his bagel. I don't know how he can stand to eat so slowly, it would be a supreme test of will for me to watch so much food—food I had already set aside for myself—linger, exposed and helpless, on its plate for so long. As it is I can barely restrain from finishing the poor bagel myself. Our friend John, I think incidentally, would have left by this time: I can see him now, within these walls, saying, "see you, guys", and walking out to his car. It seems so natural and yet I have so much trouble leaving until I have express permission to do so—and Shareep is the last person who would care particularly when I leave, or in what manner—that I always paralyze myself by wondering if now is the right moment, so of course things get done at the last moment. After all these years, I'm still looking for instruction within a machine designed by giant floating billiard balls.

I stand in the hallway as Shareep shuts the door and checks that it's locked. This is the most recent of a few times which Shareep and I have left his apartment together—I wonder what the neighbors think. I don't mention it to Shareep, as he's nearly as homophobic as I am. Though I will tell him some time, next time, probably, just as I told him about the look on the Bertucci waiter's face when Shareep told me, "I'll get the check—you get breakfast." Humanity lives funny lives; I wonder what the waiter went home to.

I hurry my good-bye so as not to make a big deal of it: "see ya Motown", and I'm off to my car. She starts first time. The white Volks, so tiny we are one being, my knees merging into the steering wheel, the sweat of my palms fusing my knuckles to the plastic, my hair pressed between the two bodies making claims on it, my head and the roof. When she turns it's as if I'm walking around a corner at fifty. It's ten past nine—Shareep, wise beyond his years, has no work ethic—so rush hour is mostly over. I drive to Manchester to look into used laptops. I find the place OK, thanks to the directions Shareep had printed last night off the Internet. There's a part of me that wanted to just try and find it, in the spirit of spontaneity, but in truth I am not very spontaneous. That's evidenced by my telling Shareep about this piddling little morning expedition in the first place—I like to get sign-off from someone, anyone, for all of my future acts.

There are three rows of used identical-looking laptops and they're all pretty much five hundred bucks. That sounds doable, as it's a nice even price, though I've no idea where I'd get the money from. A salesman begins his approach from the other end of the dilapidated store; his name is something like Isaac and he has a hunched back. He blatantly possesses a salesman's smarminess, but I don't mind. The only salesmen that irritate me are those that imply, by their bearing, their suits, and their patter, that they're better than you are, that they are offering you, in the form of a product, access to a little of the superiority that they have been granted. But all that Isaac implies is that I really, really, should buy a laptop, a point on which we are in complete agreement. Isaac doesn't have the tools at hand, really, to imply he's better than me—he's short, with a hunch and—this is territory he acquired with the job— rather greasy. He does have a likeable, techie manner, an admirable competence, but can claim ownership of no single quality that could shame me into a submissive buyer. I'm good-looking and know it. My life has been so full of 'lucky' occurrences, which—I believe, based on the evidence—resulted from my looks, I'd be an idiot to not hold some stock in them. A woman in an official position takes a liking to me, the woman whom I hope to be interested in me just happens to be exactly that, a man remembers me from five years back. And, in terms of a pure collection of shapes, I like my face. It doesn't phase me when the guy from Gentleman's Wearhouse says, "You're gonna like the way you look," because I already do. In common with Isaac, my back has a slight hunch, but I don't need to look anything near perfect since I don't have to sell anybody anything right now. In practice, on those occasions when I need to sell myself, I rarely rely much on my looks, as I'm fairly unfamiliar with their capabilities, and don't want to presume too much of the beholder.

I ask Isaac about restocking fees, then immediately regret it. I said this to raise my status from innocent customer to ball-breaking customer, but at the risk of alienating Isaac. He isn't going to sell me any laptops today (a fact he is, as yet, unaware of), but I don't want him to dislike me, because it pains me to consider anyone disliking me—especially when I'm in the room. So I'm happy when he handles the question adroitly, commenting that none of the computers would ever, in any circumstances, break, and I immediately endorse his expert opinion. Remembering the toothbrush situation, I keep a distance and speak not quite at him. The laptops looked fine—I can't tell any of them apart—and I tell Isaac I'd be back on another day to buy one. He tells me to hurry, and I assure him I will.

I know what I want to work on—my hopeless, unmarketable, raunchy campus Shakespeare adaptation comedy, but I daren't so much as look at the thing. I open my hotmail and furtively look at a few of the new ones, reading them quickly then hitting the 'x' in a panic, as though just by opening them I risk my wickedness being observed. I haven't responded to an e-mail in weeks, am scared to face what I perceive as the enormity of correspondence. There are so many things I haven't said to so many people—I'm shirking what I used to cherish, what I'm sure, on some level, I still cherish. Part of the problem is, as my reflecting glass gets more refined, it gets harder to convey myself, with all the warts and wrinkles I see and feel it's necessary to include, to others. It's been a long time since I had only a thousand words to relate to a picture; nowadays, my view of a picture is worth more words than I'm capable of generating.

I pick up a book of Latin quotes. I have always made fun of Latin as a dead language, just to poke fun at my Mum's making a career out of it, but when I was saying those things I was also thinking how I'd reserve actual judgement on Latin until I'd had some time to think about it. Now I love Latin, because it's a dead language. All the schmucks, the nothings, the salesmen, the momentary politicians that no doubt made up the large part of Rome—the men and women who were the spur of one moment or less—they've all vanished. The only people who populate the world as I travel through the city are Virgil, Cicero, Publius *et.al.*: clever, terrible, thoughtful, vibrant and passionate men. Further, these privileged few have long since been disburdened of any blemishes mortal—the frail, stale, and impalable have long since died, leaving only a small, potent core of the best electricity to pass through their heads. There are no halfway men in ancient Rome. I want to bring something out of there unaltered, and as I don't speak Latin, the most I can carry is "*Horresco Referens*". Many a story of mine will begin thus, an effort to sound clever, no doubt, but also a disclaimer. It covers more ground if I refrain from defining it.

Thursday, 8:17 a.m.—I hear a muttering and clattering of profanity and pans from somewhere downstairs: Beth's here. Shit. My Dad treats her to a cursory hello and is out the door. He timed that right. At least this time he didn't alert her to my presence, so I have a few minutes of peace. But I'm working camera at West Hartford Community T.V. today, so I must get up. I do everything that can be done upstairs first—like fishing my belt, wallet and shoes out of the pile of items disarrayed throughout my room—and then I head down for a shower.

Beth is the cleaning lady, and would be a very nice person, but for one flaw: on occasion, she has been known to come into our house and clean it. I consider this a rather unwelcome act. To me, the intrusion of strangers and near-strangers into my realm of sense perception constitutes mental clutter, which I find far more distracting and repellant than mere dust and grime. Particularly first thing in the morning, when the powers of conversation seem as far from my grasp as the powers of sorcery, I find it difficult to engage in normal communicative acts with members of the general public. To make matters worse, Beth has a nasty habit of regaling me solely with observations concerning which cleaning liquids work best, whether the vacuum is working well today, what tasks remain in her day, and how big our house is (while at the same time being relatively easy to clean). Not that I find the conversation all that uninteresting (I'm fascinated by everything, from NASCAR odds to quantum physics to tales of hide-and-go-seek): what really vexes me is that it reminds me that I'm not as middle-middle class as I, along with every other American, trusts himself to be. I mean a *cleaning lady*—can't we hide our bourgeoisie membership card a little better than that?

I pass her on the stairs. Fortunately, she doesn't throw any more at me than a brief reply to my 'Hi, how's it going?' I nibble at a breakfast, and when I hear her feet on the way downstairs, I travel upstairs, armed with another 'Hi, how's it going?' for our passing. I bolt to the shower and lock the door. She must sense something of my inner pain, for she's not yelling insignificancies at my back about cleaning products, as is her wont. I don't like the thought of her thinking that I think that I want to avoid her, as it might result in her displeasure, but it's the most comfortable of the available evils for this particular Goldilocks.

I shower, dress, get ready, am ready. I feel I can't just leave, that now I have to say something. I head down to the kitchen. I find her in the process of dropping one of our belongings on the floor. A shallow, inverted-kettle-shaped object, not sure what it's used for—butter springs to mind. She wipes it on the T-shirt stretched across her massive hip and places it back on the counter. Never again eat butter, I remind myself.

Beth is shorthaired, young, white, disheveled, very large, and Canadian. What an unfortunate place from which to be foreign: you lose benefits of being exotic but retain the 'not from round here' tag. Canada seems like a fun gig, anyway, and I don't know why you'd leave it just for another place with unscrupulous winters, where weak sunlight is conquered repeatedly by the bitter, callous dark.

Once, curious, I followed my mind as it wandered to what it might be like to bed her. An offer to drive her where she's next going (she has to take the bus), followed by an accidental hand on her knee, while reaching for the stick shift, then, if she responded accordingly, a reverse back to my house to pick up something I forgot, an invitation for her to sit on the couch while I looked for said thing, and then a clumsy pass. It's the whole standard cleaning lady scenario, the abuse of power and privilege. But even my severely underused discriminating functions, so often an accessory to the disreputable products of my imagination, are compelled to draw a line in the sand and pronounce a banishment upon looking at her. It's not that she's big, or unkempt, or of a different class. It's the way she constantly reminds me that life isn't even close to fair. And yet, beyond the complaints from the world of unusable sponges and unwashable floors, she often seems happy. I hope she is.

Beth sees I'm dressed less scrubbily than usual and rightly infers I'm on my way out. She asks what I've got on. I've got a show at ten-thirty. I look at the clock—9:04. After some quick mental arithmetic, I let her know I've a show at nine-thirty, although I'd better go early to prepare. "Oh," she says, "you've got a car now, huh?" This is true—my Mum's white Volks eyes me excitedly from the driveway. She mentions her getting the bus, and in a spurt of false generosity I ask if she'll be around in the afternoon, hinting I'd give her a lift (I do this because I know from experience she'll be gone by noon). She sputters, eventually working out the time she has to leave—around noon, to catch a bus, or one, if going by car. "No, I won't be back until after one," I apologize.

I sound awfully condescending saying this. I don't see the point in being elitist—I call and consider car park attendants, criminals, and churchgoers my equals, insofar as anyone can be rated by worth, which is a preposterous concept. But Beth brings out the uppity in me, because that's the easiest way I can distance myself from her.

It's an upset car ride because I'm thinking of my heartless and trivial-izing behavior—I applied nothing but my presence to a segment of time with another human being and was entirely unapprobrious to the moment. Did I really waste a stretch of present like that? Again? Is there any crime outside of this? I look forward instead, to redeem myself in some small way, by filling up this present moment of driving on Fern Street with happy thoughts of handing my play to a Community TV Producer. I already know the line I'll use. "I've an idea for a show, but I think it's too ambitious." The delectable mix of unconfidence, aspira-tion, and challenge that make up the statement will get them enthused, and, when they inquire, I present them with a nicely bound copy of my play, which will be a surprise, as I'd said last week—mostly truthfully, as it happens—that I didn't know what I'd do for a show, and was only there, for the moment, to learn how to use the equipment.

As I'd made an early escape from the house, I have time to begin this at the library. Time passes—it's been rarely known to fail—and I hop over to Town Hall, nervous about today's program. It's my first day as a full-fledged volunteer. I've taken a two-day training course and, as might be suspected, holding a camera for Community Television is the simplest task anyone's ever undertaken in the history of human enter-prise. You point it at the person who's speaking, then focus, then stand still for a very long time (they like to speak, these "local color"), then repeat the procedure *ad infinitum* (or until the program ends, whichever comes first). A Monkee could do it. But the whole idea that I'm responsible for someone else's show: someone else's talk and ideas, going out, as is, onto TV screens across the Greater North Main Street area—already frightens me. I step into the station's back room and Maggie's talking to a woman about "West Wing": her familiar voice immediately makes me feel better. I'm twenty minutes early, and no one should ever have anything to worry about if they're twenty minutes early. Maggie's the producer today, and like the vast majority of people who work in cable access, is incredibly nice. I guess it's just the high ratings that make the TV executives turn bad, the lingering cancer of overexposure. Maggie loves working in T.V. and with people; her husband and herself have been in the TV biz since before I can remember (though our situation is such that the longest I can possibly remember of her is a week).

The other cameraman comes in, a youngster—I'm surprised to find he's old enough to be in college (we looked older in my day), and I want to say 'hi' but he doesn't so I don't. We both act like the other isn't around, which is easy given how quiet we both are. Typical techies, we grunge about in our dirty clothes and haircuts, patiently waiting for something to happen. All I know about the show to come is that it features two politicians. One politician phones in to say he might be late; I chat with Maggie about our beat up but well-loved cars, and our hatred for driving stick in traffic jams. I'm waiting for the suitable period of producer-cameraman bonding to expire before I thrust my play at her.

The politician who warned us of his impending lateness arrives a few minutes tardy, and a few moments before the other politician. The politicians are both amiable people, friends from different constituencies, and both took care to shake my hand and the hand of my camera companion, whose name, I am absolutely pretty much positive, is George. Or maybe Gerald. Or Gary. The West Hartford politician scores points by not only asking my name but also taking care to remember it, as evidenced by his use of it in conversation two minutes after we were introduced. Nice move. At a pinch, I would have taken them for Democrats, but the New Haven one says something about himself involving the Republican party, so it turns out they're both Republican, unless the West Hartford one is a Democrat and they overcame their political differences and became—or, perhaps, remained—friends. Who cares?

I've got Camera One and I get my shot right, Maggie telling me what to do through the microphone. George, my senior in crewing terms, does the talking to the celebs, a task he relishes as little as I would. He mumbles Maggie's edicts six or seven times while the politicians courteously watch and wait for anything intelligible to exit his mouth. Then we are on. The elected speakers don't miss a beat and begin discussing the future of our country in serious tones.

I'm terrified. I see my light is on—Maggie is using my camera, so I have the entirely unwanted power to screw things up. Accompanying the terror, a curious feeling overwhelms my body: I can't find breath enough to satisfy my heart. I try taking deeper breaths through my nose, but I can't fit the necessary air through, and with each breath I seem to need more and more air, so I open my mouth. What terrifies me now is the possibility that my breathing can be heard either by the politicians or—too horrible to contemplate but I do—on the show itself. I keep my mouth and nostrils wide open in hopes that the incoming and outgoing air doesn't hit against the sides of my nose and mouth in any observable way. I look like a giant fish, with my ridiculous gaping mouth and frightened eyes. My heart is pleading for yet more air, and threatening to throw my whole body into a spasm. I try to ignore my heart. It's acting unreasonable—I'm a generally healthy young man with no history of unfortunate diseases involving involuntary muscle contractions, and all I have to do is *stand still*, for heck's sake. However, the very act of not moving, combined with the stress, is what is making my body react as it does—in my nervousness, I'm trying to shut my body down completely, stop the breath, which will, in turn, immobilize all the other functions. An object with no moving parts makes no sound, and that is what I aspire to be. Imitating George, I stand a step away from the camera, when not zooming, and keep my hands in my pockets, so that a sudden spasm of epilepsy won't tilt my camera and disrupt the proceedings. I entertain fantasies of moving freely, of running around outside, coughing loudly, singing. These clever and capable politicians—what a dolt they must think me! My breathing sounds asthmatic now, and perhaps it is. I must stay still.

I've had enough life experience to know to savor these moments of agony and terror. They are some of the best living moments we get. So I was also laughing at myself inside, and my now very real fear of panting, coughing, or experiencing a heart attack. The thirty minutes took several days to complete, and had nothing to do, as far as I was concerned, with politics. But afterwards Maggie said I was fine, and I might as well take her at her word. We chat with the politician about last night's debate. They are Democrats, I discover. They think Gore won on the issues but wore too much makeup. When they say their goodbyes, the West Hartford one again remembers my name; he's a sharp one. George left, and I said goodbye to him but quietly, for I fear his name isn't George, so it came out more like 'juh'.

I go again to the library and write in the magazine room. One man, his clothes too tight for his fleshy frame, pores over the stock prices, looking for his fortune. Poor devil. I write more of this. One in four sentences roughly approximate what I am trying to say, and one in fifty are perfection. Although their perfection isn't nearly as good as Celine's imperfection, I think I'm getting better at this. I go to the coffee shop; the goateed guy is my server. Although the only cliché bigger than a writer in a coffee shop is a goateed guy behind the bar, he looks the wise and thoughtful type. I get a small mocha to justify my presence, although I realize I'm letting three of my hoard of dollar bills, which are gathering closer together in an effort to keep their numbers from dwindling, slip away for the sake of mild chocolate flavor. I don't even get whipped cream, as I'm not in a particularly extravagant humor.

Some guy sits across from me in a ball cap. He's filling in an application and asks me what the minimum wage is. I've no idea. A short while later, our goatee approaches and says to the ball cap, "I'm going to need you to leave." The ball cap does this without argument. I've no idea.

I head back to the car. It starts first time. I remember Beth, and look at the clock. 1:10, she'll be gone. I put it in reverse. I've done four hours of what my twisted, undeserving mind will term 'work'. This merits lunch. If I'm going to get in three shifts of this, I'll need plenty of breaks.

Friday 6:54 a.m.—When I kill the alarm I'm tempted to go back to sleep, though I know my obligation tinges this possibility with awfulness. But first thing after sleep, the temptation to continue sleeping, at the expense of all other standards—those created by me and those imposed—is very, very strong. Thinking about it in the afternoon, it always seems funny how a relatively insignificant value, that of keeping up with one's sleep, can overturn the sum of promises, opportunity, long-term survival, and all the boons of awake living. The captain of my soul, while lying on my bed, is my unconscious, calling me back on the last step out of the deep.

I've always been curious about 'the first movement'. It's common knowledge, isn't it, that as soon as get that first knee or arm or hip out of the covers, the rest of the body soon follows suit, and before you know it you're in the swing of the morning rhythm. Prior to that first movement, that instant of action, my brain is sending signals to the muscle, asking me to shift my lazy keyster, but nothing gets transformed into the physical. I remember reading somewhere that the muscle actually *is* waiting for an exact number of messages—or, as the guys in the lab coats know them, neurons—from the brain to act, and this would explain why we don't throw ourselves the Eiffel Tower just because the thought crosses our mind at the top. But it always seems magical and mysterious—let's call it holy—how certain thoughts eventually manifest themselves in action. Control over one's own body is the primary expression of that miraculous triumph, mind over matter. I guess maybe that's the sort of thing T. S. Eliot's murmuring about when he goes on about the shadow, or maybe I've got it all wrong. Whatever. What I try to do now is make the first movement as small, and hence as easy, as possible. I focus on twitching my index finger a quarter of an inch. First thing in the morning, that's not as easy as it sounds.

I move—the whale breaches, the iceberg melts, the sun explodes. I turn to look at the light of my clock. Seven o' clock, the time I'm supposed to be there. I know my clock's about fifteen minutes fast and it's quarter to seven, but I need to go downstairs to confirm this, because my clock runs on a single unreliable battery. I hear dishwasher-related cluttering coming from the kitchen, the room in which the dependable clock is, and so gear myself up for a half-awake chat with a parent. This isn't so bad. Though both of my parents are teachers, our family regards mumbling as an acceptable form of communication before the first coffee. The real meaty intellectual arguments get chewed over during dinner. My family is comprised of scholars, but we are not utterly without a sense of style.

Today, it's my Mum who is downstairs moving pans around—somewhat surprising, as Mum generally wakes up seconds before she has to be out the door. She's responsible for some words heading in my direction: something like "Oh, you're going to The Children's Crumbs this morning? That's nice." My reply is instantly unmemorable. I glance at the clock on the stove and walk back up the stairs to my room.

Although I've been there the last few Fridays, I'm not entirely sure what The Children's Crumbs is. My mother has been involved with it for months, but I'm not sure she's nailed it down, either. It's a diner that seems to have some sort of affiliation with Christianity, and vaguely promotes several worthy causes. It's either a miracle in Hartford or an overly religious outlet for upper-middle class guilt, and probably both.

I help serve the coffee. I do this without pay, less out of a strong sense of compassion or religious fervor than simply because I like restaurant work. I just hope the folks there don't ask me about my morals, as I have a feeling they wouldn't find me entirely compatible. Besides, all those clever values can get in the way: if you do simple deeds well and never follow edicts, the majority of tasks will help folks out a little. More is accomplished by a cooked piece of toast than a thousand vision statements.

It's now ten to seven. It takes eight minutes to drive to the restaurant. They've got food and coffee at the restaurant so all I need is a shower. That leaves me a full ninety seconds to sleep. I go back upstairs and lie in bed, on the covers, in my nightgown. Although I now consider this a naughty residual of my morning when it was younger, innocent, and asleep, I succumb. It's awfully lazy to lie in bed for five minutes: much more so than taking a nap, because by taking a nap something gets done, but five minutes is not enough for even the accomplishment of real sleep. Normally I try to observe the maxim 'when vertical stay vertical'—this must sound great in Latin—but I never manage to keep this up very long. I take out a Beller book so I don't feel so bad about being on empty. Life isn't bad here, between book and bed.

When I finish becoming ready I'm late; I feel guilty, as this could have been avoided. I assumed I'd have to move my parents' cars out of the driveway, but Mum, bless her, has already done that for me. My Mum has long since ascended to what I call 'a higher state of politeness'. Beyond minding 'p's and 'q's, politeness depends entirely on a delicate intelligence. Socially stupid people cannot be truly polite, not necessarily due to any innate meanness, but merely because they neither try nor succeed to fathom others' needs. I'm quite stupid in this regard, but I hope someday to learn. The golden rule is a primitive kingdom, good as an occasional fallback, but no basis for a real philosophy of social action. It's not fit to base a dinner party on, let alone a just state. But then, I've never met anyone remotely like Kant.

It's dark and drizzly on the roads and I try to focus on getting there safely, not hitting the car ahead or behind me. I note how we're all trying to make sure we don't meet, as would happen if our cars bumped. If we were to be forced out of our cars to exchange numbers, we'd have nothing to contribute to each other's lives except hassle, and so we steer clear of one another.

Up ahead, incredibly, a man is walking towards us carrying a tree strapped diagonally across his back. It's considerably larger than he is, what in another season I'd call a Christmas tree. The tree is impossibly gigantic behind his broad shoulders. Walking through the mist is a demigod, how did this slice of the underworld appear at half past six in the suburbs? I'm sleepily excited—I've reached that part of the story where anything can happen, where the real is suspended and oft flies away.

I get nearer, and now our tree-man is just a tree, behind a lamppost, bent on its hill. So it wasn't real, not for the other drivers, although it was a real event in my mind—and what is a world without a mind? How can I say it didn't happen, in the same way that walking and talking, and remembering thus, happen? For a couple of years now, since taking up writing as a serious matter, my dreams and reality have begun to merge a little—certain past memories are indefinable in status, there's no way for me to determine if they were within dreams or without. I know this is how they define psychosis, and furthermore, since my dreams usually don't feature me, multiple personality syndrome. But I'm eager to explore this blending of myself and everything else, for I intimate within this journey some kind of simple, actual immortality (As real as breath, as natural as being, as fantastic as tomorrow), a freedom from individual identity and thus death, and I'm excited about finding what this is and what it means. Joyce, Socrates, Woolf—what was death to these folks? Lou Reed puts great spiritual significance to 'It's all right,' and I, too, think there's something casually absolute about our existence.

As I enter the city, I witness the rain complimenting the cracks and fissures of the pavement. Hartford is beautiful as always—abandoned, wary, desperate. It's the only beautiful place of its ugly county, save the odd farm, the only place not sanitized hideously against memory. The sign outside the car park carries huge red stencil saying 'Early Bird Special—$5'. I don't have to pay because I'm clergy. I take a ticket and park.

At the restaurant a dignified, white-haired man stands behind the counter. It's Bob (See? I really am melting into everybody), a first-time volunteer, and Joe is keeping him busy with making coffee. I try to hide my disappointment: coffee's the one thing I do really well around here. Bob has a voice like in the Bogart movies, resonant, beautiful, and nonchalant.

Joe's in a good mood as he greets us from the kitchen. He asks me how I am and cares about the answer. We're on good terms now—I called him Al by mistake on my first day, an indiscretion which led to a tiny glimmer of distaste that evaporated within minutes. Joe is a large man with a ponytail, big and calm enough to pass for a mobster. He's also hugely, unobtrusively, and obviously good, a goodness that radiates without effort or pride. Were Christ around today he'd be an Apostle. As it is, he works in the kitchen and manages the running of the restaurant. Food and taxes, mostly, books and bread.

Bob is asking me (Bob the younger) how to do things, and I'm uncomfortable telling a man thrice my age how to work a diner, particularly as I haven't been here that many times myself. So I try to position myself near the kitchen so that when Joe comes out I might catch his eye and inspire him to unload some menial task on me. I love menial tasks and am thrilled when I get to wipe down the trays or load the bagels. Of course, that's partly because I only work there for two hours once a week, and in that short span of time the joy of things getting done doesn't lose its charm.

The customers begin to trickle in, many of them familiar—the one with the Rick Moranis voice; the one who looks like a Minstrel (I hate myself for thinking this); the friendly suit, who, by the look of him, can only possibly work in insurance; the one who always looks impatient and I don't know why he puts up with us. Bob, more capable then he humbly pretends to be, has things well under control, so I go fold the silverware into the lunch napkins. This process results in those paper serviettes you find in every restaurant. Catherine taught me how to do this and, along with the increasing ability to stitch a sentence, it's the one skill, I like to think, that sets me apart from the crowd. I must admit that one of the reasons I go fold napkins is to work on something that Bob doesn't yet know how to do, to boost my status in his eyes. I interpret his silence as proof of my success. Soon I'm lost in my own world, the succession of completed napkins a comfortable and recurring accomplishment.

Bob leaves as soon as Catherine and Pete show up. Pete works the kitchen; he's one of the few guys who can say "How ya doin'" and get away with it, and he's not yet thirty—already he gets respect. He used to work catering for The Boss ("Yeah he's really down-to-earth. Doesn't like scalpers though."). Cathy is the full-time, paid counter person, and unlike us volunteers actually knows what she's doing. I'm free to go but I stick around, because I like Cathy and I want to give the impression that I'm helping out. Also, Cathy's a big hugger and I sort of want of hug. She hugged me the first time and always hugs manager Bob (everyone here is named Bob, supporting either my deepening psychosis or the theory that the restaurant-cum-charity is some strange conforming cult) when she sees him off. I feel a bit perverted, waiting for a hug from a full-figured black co-worker with two kids and a boyfriend. It's not sexual: not that Cathy couldn't be attractive to me, but there's far too wide a gulf of circumstance to even consider a pairing. I just get jealous sometimes of those people who live huggy-kissy lifestyles. I always appear standoffish and awkward—this is mainly because I *am* standoffish and awkward—and the only people who hug and kiss me are forward, needy types. I don't want forward, needy types to hug and kiss me (for these hugs and kisses always entail a commitment, as if their testimony to my kissable worthiness makes me a lifelong ally to their every whim); I want casual, chic friends to embrace me upon meeting, as they would if we both knew how to be French.

But Catherine's in the kitchen and in the midst of a conversation with Pete, so I head out, waving to Joe as I open the door. There's a white girl outside smoking whom I recognize—she's been a customer, a charming and crazy girl who laughed as we murdered all the details of her order, while Pete sat nearby and called her 'sweetheart' every chance he got. I don't know why she's smoking outside the restaurant; she hasn't come in yet today. There's a harried look on her face, but I say nothing—the only words I've said to her during our co-existence are "for here or to go?"

It's the same car park attendant as ever, a skinny black gentleman who looks remarkably like the vampire in the Ray-Ban ads. We have a ritual, wherein I say, "I'm from The Children's Crumbs?" and he replies, "From the church?" and although this is not technically true, I say "Yeah," because this is what I'm supposed to say. Sometimes he has me sign the back of my ticket and sometimes he doesn't, but in either case he lets me go for free. This time I say "How ya doing?" as a real question, for I'm sure he recognizes me now, and I don't want to belittle his patent intelligence by assuming he doesn't. He does, and takes my ticket, but then I spoil everything by saying, "from the church?" just to make sure I'm in the clear. There's a trace of irritation as he takes my ticket and lets me go. I'm ashamed of myself as I put the clutch in—I had a real chance to do things right, the little, ever-so-important things, and instead I needlessly pissed off a car park attendant with a more fully-developed sense of social discretion. Well, we get most things wrong in this life.

I'm contemplating a brief excursion to Barnes & Noble—one-dollar tea and free water—but then I remember it's rush hour and to go on the highway would amount to spiritual suicide. So I take Asylum Avenue, all the way to home.

I let Tess out the back but we both think twice about the drizzle and claw for the door moments later. I write this. I'll begin to type it soon. It seems an elaborately arduous process, scribing and then typing, but it lets me write it from scratch a second time. If I were just to revise it from a screen my eyes would just skim the whole thing, and I'd avoid revising the parts I despise the most. But when I have to read over the whole thing, there's more possibility I'll be forced to do something with the unwanted bits, or—still a lesser possibility, due to my immaturity—discard them altogether. I go upstairs to type, praying to myself that the altitude shift would induce a more elevated standard of prose. Closer to the gods, and further from the dead—although the dead have probably, it must be said, more great stories to their credit, all told.

I run over in my mind whom to send it to. Valerie, certainly: Spark (I must read more of her, I got so much out of a few hours' reading) taught me the trick of writing to somebody, and she's more or less whom I wrote this to. But I might as well send it to a few other friends as well, even if there are sections I'm slightly ashamed about. Because I think I should try and 'live an honest life'. For some reason that phrase has become associated with the absence of cruel deeds and thoughts, as espousing a cautioned, positive simplicity, and I don't understand why. The whole truth is more useful than nothing but. Essential to anyone's story is the counterpoint, the sun's shadow, and the guy who works the soil and shares himself with others must live that part of him that his conscience (in washing his hands in the evening) hides, if he is to be honest. I'll pepper everything I serve with failure and heartbreak and sin. If these aren't a part of your story, you're either a liar, or too young to write worth a damn.

I fall asleep before I finish, and hate myself for it. But Friday night, which will be crazy, deserves its groundwork, and if I keep trying to move forward I'll never get anywhere.

Another Day at Oxford

◆

One of my favorite stories about you, Dad,
was when
a friend of yours—
I don't remember who—
told us about the time
he visited you at Oxford.

You showed him round, of course.
The ancient walls, the gardens.
With the customary handshakes and chit-chat,
you introduced him to each of the faculty.
Dr. So-and-so,
Dr. So-and so.

You also introduced him to the cleaning lady,
a quiet woman from
Russia, but there was no
also
about it.
A worker at the college,

the cleaning lady was no less important
than the dean.

She was embarrassed about her lack
of English,
but knowing you, you apologized
for knowing even less Russian.
you gave the time
to discuss with your friend
and your co-worker
some of the responsibilities
that make up
her job.
You brought him to the stairs she polished
(a chapter from a history textbook).
You pointed out the floor she cleaned
(a law tutorial).
You lauded her work, because
it was good work.

When the anecdote ended,
you said, "Well, she worked as hard as anybody there.
Probably harder.
She certainly worked harder than I did."

It's a good story, a good
thing that happened.
I've told it a couple times.
I think I should, with
people who are trying to get to know me,
and who I want to get to know me,
people who are trying to figure out what makes me tick,

where I'm coming from.
Well,
that's where I'm coming from.

One Drink, One Candy

◆

There was a structure to life then.
Not the blocked-off time, but
the way there were
three bowls of sugar cereal at breakfast,
then teeth brushing,
just as teeth were brushed
at the end of the day.

When we went for a walk,
we'd go to Liggett's[1],
and the custom, your custom
 was I and my brothers each
could choose one drink,
one dessert[2].

---

1 I applied there one summer out of college,
    but they didn't want me. Or I might not have
    handed in the application.
    Which-ever.
2 This originated with the 'one fruit, one dessert'
    after-dinner rule. Granny Smiths
    and ice cream is a good example.

Cherry Coke, Mountain Dew, Sprite.
Runts, those apple pies with the nasty *faux* sugar coating, Bounty bars.

Then we'd go to Westmoor Park, look at
the tame animals.
Maybe feed them
some grass, which was a bit
pointless, because
if there was one thing they had
on their side of the fence,
it was grass.
Then we'd walk through the forest.
It was a small forest, and we
knew where most of the paths led—
where the river widened, where the reeds got thick, the best place
to look for walking sticks, the bridge.
We'd play pooh sticks, dropping the bits of wood,
and running to the other side to see
who won.
There was a spooky cabin which no-one seemed to use.
A lot of times we'd have a ball or frisbee with us, so we'd
throw it around the open field,
the one with the hill and the flagpole.

Somewhere in the middle of all that,
Each of us kids would have our drink,
and our dessert.
We gave the two their own moments, so that
pleasure was evenly spaced
over its time.

Westmoor Park[3] was cool because
it had everything you could possibly have
in the world:
a forest,
a river,
animals,
a wide open field.

And us, of course.

---

3 I went back there this past
   summer, with Claire and Munish.
   It was boiling American hot, and
   we couldn't find the Pooh Stick bridge, and
   they were griping at me. So much
   for nostalgia. Driving out, we passed
   Bennett and his Dad, who live
   nearby. Bennett hopped in
   and we went to Mike's drug store (not
   Liggett's but the other one).
   Mike was doing fine.

Opposing Sides

━━━━━━━━━━━ ◆ ━━━━━━━━━━━

CHARACTERS:
JOE, an American spy
PHRISKEDANNIA, a Balvissian spy.

(A wall, of a height convenient for sitting, is in the center of the stage. In front of the wall is what appears to be a bundle of clothes.)

(JOE, tired, walks in from offstage. He lies on the wall, takes his jacket off and covers himself with it. He tries to go to sleep but is uncomfortable and keeps fidgeting. Giving up on the wall idea, he stands up and walks to the bundle of clothes. He pokes it to ensure that it's soft, and then lies down, using the bundle as a pillow. A moment later, the bundle jumps up and sparks to life. It is PHRISKEDANNIA, lying under his jacket. As both stand up anxiously, the jackets remain on the ground.)

PHRISKEDANNIA: *(in Balvissian)* Keliatta Schrep! Okhai-nerr! Fescher chrum paddaweptos?

JOE: *(in Balvissian, haltingly)* Kola…Hadai narfolo…candiesta narfolo hadai…wenteb.
PHRISKEDANNIA: *(In Balvissian)* Chesta Bolvizzi? Balai…
JOE: No, no, I'm American. Listen, do you speak English?
PHRISKEDANNIA: Sure, I speak English.
JOE: Could we speak English? I know I'm supposed to know Balvissian, but the training was really rushed, and…
PHRISKEDANNIA: Of course. You are American?
JOE: *(nods)* You Balvissian?
PHRISKEDANNIA: Yes.

(Pause. JOE sits on a wall, gestures to his left.)

JOE: Have a seat.
PHRISKEDANNIA: *(not moving)* Nice weather we're having.
JOE: Yeah, just peachy.

(Long pause, Joe removes CIGARETTE PACK from his shirt pocket, lights cigarette and takes drags, PHRISKEDANNIA observing. Finally, JOE stands up and extends his hand.)

JOE: Name's Joseph. Call me Joe.
PHRISKEDANNIA: *(Approaches JOE, shakes his hand.)* Phriskedannia.
JOE: Nice name.
PHRISKEDANNIA: It means—
JOE: Wait, wait! Shoot, I know this. Hold on. Phris-ke…what did you say?
PHRISKEDANNIA: Dannia.
JOE: Right, right. Phriskedannia. Big house…with feisty roosters?
PHRISKEDANNIA: *(laughs)* It means peace.
JOE: Sorry. My Balvissian needs some work.
PHRISKEDANNIA: Think nothing of it. Call me Danny.
JOE: Sure thing, Danny.

(Pause.)

JOE: *(Slowly, sounding it out.)* Phriskedannia. Peace. Aren't you in the wrong profession, Danny?

PHRISKEDANNIA: You know what profession I am in?

JOE: Same as mine. *(beat)* You're a spy.

PHRISKEDANNIA : You won't believe I'm a simple farmer?

JOE: No. All the farmers got out of this dump a long time ago. Only us spies left, my friend.

PHRISKEDANNIA: Maybe I'm a traditional farmer. Too stubborn to get off my land.

JOE: Couldn't be.

PHRISKEDANNIA: How do you know? You think us farmers can't speak English?

JOE: You're wearing traditional farmer's clothes.

PHRISKEDANNIA: *(looking down at his outfit)* Yes, I am. So?

JOE: Traditional farmers wear Wrangler's Jeans and Nike sweaters. The only people who wear   traditional farmer's clothes are spies who are trying to look like traditional farmers.

PHRISKEDANNIA: I told the agency they shouldn't use these outfits.

JOE: They should have listened to you.

(PHRISKEDANNIA paces a few steps stage right.)

PHRISKEDANNIA: Why do you say I'm in the wrong profession?

JOE: Your name. Phriskedannia. Peace.

PHRISKEDANNIA: I work for peace.

JOE: Yeah, and I work for the Easter Bunny.

PHRISKEDANNIA: Tell him I say hello.

JOE: Next time he invites me to Washington, I will.

(*PHRISKEDANNIA walks to where his and Joe's jackets lie on the floor. He picks them both up, and places them carefully on the wall, several feet from where JOE is sitting. PHRISKEDANNIA places his jacket closer to JOE than JOE's jacket. PHRISKEDANNIA takes a couple of steps forward, away from the jacket, and begins to pace four or five steps back and forth. JOE watches all this intently.*)

PHRISKEDANNIA: So I guess I'm supposed to kill you.

JOE: I guess so. Cigarette?

PHRISKEDANNIA: Yeah, thanks. (*Takes cigarette, JOE lights it. Resumes pacing.*) Or you could kill me. That could happen, too.

JOE: It could happen.

PHRISKEDANNIA: It's a possibility.

JOE: It's a possibility. So which is it to be?

PHRISKEDANNIA: Are there only two possibilities?

JOE: I don't know. Are there?

PHRISKEDANNIA: Not necessarily.

JOE: Continue.

PHRISKEDANNIA: We could both kill each other. Or—we could both kill ourselves. We both die, in either case.

JOE: What would be the point of that?

PHRISKEDANNIA: I don't know. I just think it's important to mention all the possibilities.

JOE: Would there be a point to that?

PHRISKEDANNIA: No.

JOE: Well, then…

PHRISKEDANNIA: (*stops pacing*) Another possibility is that neither of us die.

JOE: Is that a genuine possibility?

(*Pause while PHRISKEDANNIA thinks, then he resumes pacing.*)

PHRISKEDANNIA: No.

JOE: Ah.

PHRISKEDANNIA: But worth mentioning, all the same. Always list the possibilities.

JOE: Even if they are impossible?

PHRISKEDANNIA: Until we list them, we don't know that.

JOE: You know, the 'me killing you' option is becoming increasingly attractive.

PHRISKEDANNIA: Hold on. we haven't even listed all the possibilities yet.

JOE: What other possibilities are there?

PHRISKEDANNIA: Let me think.

(Pause. PHRISKEDANNIA keeps pacing.)

JOE: Come up with anything?

PHRISKEDANNIA: *(Counting on his fingers)* You die, I die, we both live, we both die. No, that's all the possibilities, I believe.

(PHRISKEDANNIA sits down, stares into space. JOE flicks cigarette.)

PHRISKEDANNIA: Unless we both walk away from here.

JOE: You just said that wasn't a possibility.

PHRISKEDANNIA: I said that neither of us dying wasn't a possibility. After all, we all die some time. *(Beat. Turns toward JOE.)* But neither of us dying *right now*—surely we can consider that.

JOE: You know we can't.

PHRISKEDANNIA: Why?

JOE: Both of us walk away? Toodle-oo? Nobody kills anybody?

PHRISKEDANNIA: Yes.

JOE: We can't do that.

PHRISKEDANNIA: Nobody gets killed. *(pointing)* You walk over there, I walk over here. *(sotto voice)* We both say we have never met. *(Gives overemphasized wink.)*

JOE: Well, that's great, Danny, *(Returns PHRISKEDANNIA's wink in mockery.)* but we *have* met, and now we both have our jobs to do. And you can walk that way if you want, but if you do, I'll be right behind you. And it won't be to talk about the weather.

PHRISKEDANNIA: Do you hate me?

JOE: I don't hate anyone. Except the Yankees. But we're in a war here. Look around. Fact is, you and I are enemies. Now, I don't mean that in a bad way. You seem like a nice guy, Danny, and it's nice talking with you. But some time today I'm gonna have to do my job. If you kill me first, fine. And maybe I'll kill you. But if I leave this spot and no one's dead, well—I haven't done my job. And I'm not going to let that happen.

PHRISKEDANNIA: You're a very cheerful person, Joe, you know that?

(JOE grinds his cigarette into the ground with his foot as he speaks)

JOE: Look, this isn't easy for me, and I'm sure it ain't easy for you. But we're both trained professionals. Aren't we? We know what we're doing. We know why we signed up. Am I right?

PHRISKEDANNIA: I suppose you are right.

JOE: I mean, could you really—are you telling me, you could just turn around, chicken out—

PHRISKEDANNIA: "Chicken out"?

JOE: Yeah, chicken out. Run away, like a chicken.

(PHRISKEDANNIA stands up, discarding cigarette, and runs a few steps stage right, imitating a chicken.)

PHRISKEDANNIA: I like this! This is not so bad!

(PHRISKEDANNIA turns around as about to chicken run by JOE, but JOE, irritated, stands up and grabs him by the shirt.)

JOE: You're just going to let an American spy slip through your fingertips?
PHRISKEDANNIA: *(looking at his hands)* You're a bit big for my finger—
JOE: *(exploding a little)* You know what I mean!

(JOE lets go of PHRISKEDANNIA. PHRISKEDANNIA, somewhat in shock, looks at JOE for an instant, then sits on the ground and sighs.)

PHRISKEDANNIA: Yes, you're right. Of course you are right. If I was to "chicken out", as you say, I could not go home. Maybe I could lie to my agency, even my family—but in the end I could not lie to myself. This *(Motioning around himself with his arms.)* is what I do. I am a spy and I have promised to follow my country. Just as you have. We must both accept our duty.

(JOE sits back on wall and puts head on hand pensively. PHRISKEDANNIA stands up, puts his hand on JOE's shoulder.)

PHRISKEDANNIA: I'm sorry, Joe. It was unprofessional of me to suggest such things. Of course, we must do what we must do. Please forgive me.
JOE: Forget about it.
PHRISKEDANNIA: No, I insist.
JOE: No, I mean forget about it. It's all right, that's what I mean. Sorry I snapped at you. That was unprofessional, too.

(Pause. PHRISKEDANNIA retakes his spot on the wall.)

PHRISKEDANNIA: I guess we are both pretty unprofessional spies.

(JOE smiles. Pause.)

PHRISKEDANNIA: So, Joe, tell me about yourself.

JOE: *(Looks at PHRISKEDANNIA in disbelief.)* Well, I'm a CIA operative, taking a delightful stroll through war-torn Balvissia, and now I'm having a little chat with a Balvissian agent, who will probably, I assume, kill me if I don't kill him. That about covers it. Anything else you want to know? My star sign, maybe?

PHRISKEDANNIA: I already knew all that.

JOE: You think I'm gonna tell you state secrets?

PHRISKEDANNIA: What movies do you like?

JOE: That's your idea of interrogation?

PHRISKEDANNIA: I'm not interrogating.

JOE: I don't think my taste in movies is very important to either of us right now.

PHRISKEDANNIA: Maybe, maybe not. *(Stands up, crosses downstage left)* They say, as Rome burned, Nero played the fiddle. In the middle of our biggest crises, that is when art is most necessary.

JOE: Nero was crazy. He burned the place himself.

PHRISKEDANNIA: I'd rather be crazy then think about war.

JOE: War pays your paycheck.

PHRISKEDANNIA: Yes, but I'm on a break right now. *(Wondering if the phrase is right.)* 'Coffee break?'

JOE: *(pause)* 'Goodfellas' was a good movie…

PHRISKEDANNIA: I didn't see that. I liked…oh, 'Life is Beautiful'!

JOE: Didn't see it. *(Stands up.)* Well, it's great chatting with you, Danny, it really is. Now can we get back to figuring out who's killing who?

PHRISKEDANNIA: Oh, I know—'Titanic'. You must have seen that.

JOE: Sure. The wife made me see it.

PHRISKEDANNIA: Did you like it?

JOE: It sucked. Boat hits iceberg, boat sinks. That's your movie. Hope I didn't spoil it for you.

PHRISKEDANNIA: Oh, I saw it already. I thought it was very good.

JOE: *(beat)* How come?

PHRISKEDANNIA: The pictures, the…images. Romance in a world that is not working any more. The acting was—too Hollywood, it's true, so I stopped listening, and then I am just looking at two young people who love each other, on a boat that will never find its land. And—when they are kissing—all that water, everywhere, taking over the situation. Very sad—but beautiful. It was very pleasant to my eyes.

JOE: It was very pleasant to my eyes too. They caught up on their sleep.

(Pause. Then JOE, ready for business, walks toward jackets, and picks them both up. He moves towards PHRISKEDANNIA, to hand him his jacket.)

JOE: So—

(PHRISKEDANNIA waves JOE off with his hand, walks by him to the wall, and sits down.)

PHRISKEDANNIA: Not yet, Joe.

JOE: I'm sorry?

PHRISKEDANNIA: Give me some minutes. Just one or two. I know we have to do—that, and I will be ready to do it, but right now, I just want to look at that tree over there, just look at it, for two minutes. Is that OK?

JOE: *(beat)* OK. Sure, Danny. That's OK.

(JOE puts both jackets back, sits back down, this time on PHRISKEDANNIA's left. Both look offstage in the same direction, at the tree.)

JOE: Hey, you know what this is like. *(beat)* Waiting for Godot.
PHRISKEDANNIA: So am I Vladimir or Estragon?
JOE: Huh?
PHRISKEDANNIA: Am I Vladimir or Estragon?
JOE: Oh, don't know. Never read it.
PHRISKEDANNIA: I guess that makes me Vladimir then.
JOE: I was supposed to read it. 10th Grade, Mrs. Evans' class. I was too
    busy trying to impress Helen Wakowski.
PHRISKEDANNIA: Was she pretty?
JOE: *(smiles)* Was she pretty? *(beat)* No. No, she wasn't, actually. I was
    in high school. I would have hit on a toaster oven if I thought it
    was giving me the eye.
PHRISKEDANNIA: That's a joke, I understand.
JOE: Yes, that's a joke. I wonder where she is now. Helen Wakowski. She
    did have nice eyes. Bright green. These high school romances are
    funny, huh? You spend all this time thinking about a girl, won-
    dering if she likes you, trying to figure out what you can get away
    with—and you're not sure what you *want* to get away with, since
    you're sixteen and you don't have a clue what you're doing. Now I
    don't even know what town she lives in. It's not like I was in love
    with the girl, but still—I don't know the first thing about her now.
    Isn't that weird? That I felt all that then, and now I don't know
    anything about her?
PHRISKEDANNIA: I know quite a bit about my 'high school romance':
    she's my wife.
JOE: Really?
PHRISKEDANNIA: We grew up in the same village. She was born two
    months after me. I always knew—well, when you're six years old

you don't know about these things, but I knew—I knew she would always be near me. Somehow…I could not imagine her not close to me, in my life. *(beat)* I still cannot imagine it.

JOE: You really grew up in a village?

PHRISKEDANNIA: Is that so strange?

JOE: With little houses, and village fairs, and cows and stuff like that?

PHRISKEDANNIA: Well, a cow, yes. More goats then cows.

JOE: We don't have villages where I come from. We have towns without major shopping malls, but that whole 'met my wife in the village' thing—that only happens in Manhattan. Well, I guess you would-n't exactly meet your *wife* in the Village either.

PHRISKEDANNIA: I don't understand.

JOE: *(waving his hand)* Never mind; it's not important.

PHRISKEDANNIA: Are you married, Joe?

(Pause. JOE looks uncomfortable.)

PHRISKEDANNIA: I'm sorry, I should not…don't answer that, it's personal, and we're both…spies, so—

JOE: Yes, I'm married. *(Stands up, walks a few steps upstage right.)* You told me, so it's only fair I tell you.

(Pause. JOE looks offstage, in his own world. PHRISKEDANNIA gets up and walks towards jackets, reaches in a pocket. JOE, suddenly noticing this and thinking he's reaching for his gun, grabs PHRISKEDANNIA's arm violently. JOE slowly pulls PHRISKEDANNIA's arm out, to reveal PHRISKEDANNIA's wallet grasped in his hand.)

PHRISKEDANNIA: It's not a gun! It's not a gun!

JOE: Jesus! Tell me next time.

PHRISKEDANNIA: I want to show you something.

(*PHRISKEDANNIA pulls out a photo, hands it proudly to* Joe.)

JOE: These your real kids?
PHRISKEDANNIA: I'm sorry...what?
JOE: These your real kids?
PHRISKEDANNIA: Of course!
JOE: *(handing photo back)* You should be careful. You know, the CIA doesn't let us carry photos of our real kids.
PHRISKEDANNIA: Why not?
JOE: Just in case you're ever captured and killed. Makes sure other intelligence agencies can't go after your families and torture them.

(*PHRISKEDANNIA, very deliberately, puts his photo back in his wallet and pockets both in his front pants pocket.*)

PHRISKEDANNIA: Why would they do that?
JOE: *(shrugs)* All kinds of sick freaks out there. *(He takes WALLET out of his pants pocket and opens it for PHRISKEDANNIA.)* Well, you showed me yours, so here's mine.
PHRISKEDANNIA: But they're not—
JOE: Not mine. That's right. But if they were, this one *(pointing)* would be Frederick, and this one would be Anna. And that's my wife, Cindy.
PHRISKEDANNIA: A beautiful family.
JOE: They sure are. Shame they're not mine. *(Puts wallet back in his pocket.)* Anna and Frederick   are ugly little runts, really.
PHRISKEDANNIA: *(apologetically)* Oh...But I'm sure—
JOE: Oh, only kidding, they're good kids. Miss them every day.
PHRISKEDANNIA: Yes, I miss my children, too. *(beat)* So that other photo—actors?

JOE: *(beat)* You can keep this a secret?

PHRISKEDANNIA: I will keep this a secret. You can trust me absolutely.

JOE: I know. Those kids belong to another agent I know from head-quarters. Let's call him Jim Brown. My kids and my wife posed with him in his photo.

PHRISKEDANNIA: But that is not his real name, of course.

JOE: Of course not. His real name's Jim Grey.

PHRISKEDANNIA: You are not supposed to tell me that!

JOE: *(laughing)* It's O.K. Jim doesn't bother much with protocol, and neither do I. He wouldn't mind.

PHRISKEDANNIA: This Jim Grey is a friend of yours?

JOE: *(nods)* Nice guy and a darn fine Ping-Pong player. Promise you won't torture his family?

PHRISKEDANNIA: If you insist.

(JOE takes his pack of cigarettes out from his shirt pocket.)

JOE: Another cigarette?

PHRISKEDANNIA: Oh! Thank you. *(Reaches in pack.)* Oh no, I couldn't. It's your last cigarette!

JOE: It's OK. I got another pack. *(Taps jacket pocket.)*

PHRISKEDANNIA: It's very kind of you.

(PHRISKEDANNIA takes cigarette out; it's in the pack back-wards. He holds it up between his fingertips.)

PHRISKEDANNIA: Hey!

JOE: What?

PHRISKEDANNIA: *(holding cigarette)* This cigarette! You put it in upside down! You do that thing!

JOE: That thing?

PHRISKEDANNIA: You turn the last cigarette upside down! *(excitedly, miming)* When you open a new pack, you take a cigarette out, flip it over, and put it back in. Then you save it until the end. The lucky cigarette!

JOE: *(lighting PHRISKEDANNIA's cigarette)* You know the drill.

PHRISKEDANNIA: You let me have your lucky cigarette. You *are* an unprofessional spy!

> *(As JOE and PHRISKEDANNIA speak, JOE throws the first pack on the ground, reaches into his jacket pocket, gets a new pack, takes the wrapper off, throws it on the ground, taps the pack a few times to spread the nicotine, then opens the pack, takes a cigarette out, flips it over, and turns it back in.)*

JOE: Well, it wasn't very lucky. It got us into this mess, didn't it? I shouldn't smoke, really, anyway. I don't know if you heard the news? There's been some lawsuits over in the U.S. Apparently these things are bad for you.

PHRISKEDANNIA: You're kidding. And here I am, smoking ten cigarettes a day purely for my health.

JOE: Came as a shock to me too.

> *(Joe takes a different cigarette out, lights it, puts pack in his shirt pocket.)*

PHRISKEDANNIA: *(enjoying his cigarette)* Ah. Very nice. *(pause)* So how should we...

> *(Silence. JOE smokes.)*

PHRISKEDANNIA: How should we...do...this thing?

JOE: You mean-

PHRISKEDANNIA: Yes. That's what I mean. Yes.

(Pause.)

JOE: Well, we could take ten paces, turn around, fire…
PHRISKEDANNIA: The old way, yes? The old-fashioned way?
JOE: What do you think?

(PHRISKEDANNIA paces.)

PHRISKEDANNIA: The only thing is…
JOE: Yes?
PHRISKEDANNIA: Would you walk all ten paces? Or would you turn around early, shoot me in the back?
JOE: Would you?
PHRISKEDANNIA: Yes, I think I would. Yes, I'm afraid that I think I would. I might. *(beat)* Standing here, talking to you, you know, I *want* to go ten paces, but when I'm actually there—I'd be so scared, so…*(Makes motion with hands.)* boiling up inside, that— well, I think that I would go eight, or maybe nine paces, *(miming it)* and then turn around and fire. I'm sorry, but I should tell you that. Eight or nine paces.
JOE: In that case, I'll go six or seven.

(Both laugh. PHRISKEDANNIA snaps his fingers, inspired.)

PHRISKEDANNIA: We could do it like your old cowboy movies! *(Crouches like a gunslinger, cigarette in mouth.)* Two cowboys, facing off. Staring at each other. *(Pulls hands up as if to shoot.)* Pow! Pow!
JOE: Easy there, pardner.

PHRISKEDANNIA: *(in a Western accent)* How 'bout it, Mr. Cowboy?

JOE: I'm from the East Coast. I'm no cowboy.

PHRISKEDANNIA: You know how to fire a gun, right? It's perfect!

JOE: I'm not a quick draw.

PHRISKEDANNIA: Neither am I!

JOE: How do I know that?

PHRISKEDANNIA: How do I know that *you* are not a quick draw? But let's just see how it goes. Just for practice.

(PHRISKEDANNIA helps JOE up and ushers him, by the elbow, to a spot stage left. He begins walking away from JOE across the stage.)

PHRISKEDANNIA: You stand here, and I…

(PHRISKEDANNIA has stopped quite far away stage right, so he has to raise his voice.)

PHRISKEDANNIA:…am standing here! *(Drops his cigarette, stamps on it. Yelling.)* Are you ready?

JOE: *(panicky)* Wait, this is just practice, right?

PHRISKEDANNIA: You are ready?

JOE: *(His cigarette drops out of his mouth. Yelling.)* Wait, no guns, right? No guns? *(Taps his side and makes 'gun' sign with his hands.)*

(PHRISKEDANNIA is now driven to a panic by JOE's noise and motions. Both look ready to fire now, but neither appears keen.)

PHRISKEDANNIA: No guns! No guns! *(Waves left hand; his right stays by his side.)* Hands!

JOE: *(Waving his left hand wildly.)* Hands up! Hands up!

(PHRISKEDANNIA and JOE slowly, slowly lift their right hands up, until both have both hands above their head. They laugh and approach each other, hands still up. Upon reaching each other, they clasp hands excitedly, relieved.)

PHRISKEDANNIA: Perhaps that was not the best idea.

(JOE lies down on wall, exhausted.)

JOE: Next time you have an idea—try thinking first.

(As they talk, JOE sits up, gets out his cigarettes, gives one to PHRISKEDANNIA, then to himself, lights them.)

JOE: Thought that was going to be my last cigarette back there. You didn't even give me time to finish it.

PHRISKEDANNIA: Sorry. *(Sits down.)* Let us at least make death polite, yes? Not like that, all that running like chickens. Most people die that way, not knowing at all what is going on. We—one of us, that is—do not have to.

(Pause.)

PHRISKEDANNIA: We are killers, but at least we finish our cigarettes.

(Pause. Both smoke.)

PHRISKEDANNIA: I know I cannot ask you if you have ever killed anyone.

(Silence from JOE.)

PHRISKEDANNIA: In training, we had to stab bags of potatoes, *(motioning)* slit where the throats would be, you understand? And we had to imagine they were people. *(pause)* It was not so hard. I thought it would be hard. But it wasn't.

(Pause.)

PHRISKEDANNIA: Do you like your job, Joe?
JOE: *(shrugs)* It's a living.

(PHRISKEDANNIA laughs.)

PHRISKEDANNIA: Yes. Yes, it is a living. Maybe not for the people we must kill, but for us, yes? It's a living!

(Pause.)

PHRISKEDANNIA: We should determine what we are going to do about...the body.
JOE: *(disinterested)* If you want to.
PHRISKEDANNIA: If it's me, I don't want to be *(indicating vaguely with his hand)* here too long. I think maybe there are birds that might eat at my face, and I don't want that to happen. My family will see me—you know. They will see me at the funeral.
JOE: OK. I'll tie your jacket around your face so the birds can't get at you. Then I'll call my contact, and he'll be here in a couple of hours. Is that soon enough?
PHRISKEDANNIA: Oh, sure. That will be fine. No problem. *(pause)* You're not worried what happens for you? If...if it's you?
JOE: I trust you.
PHRISKEDANNIA: I won't leave you here to be eaten by the birds, Joe—

JOE: I'm sure you won't.

PHRISKEDANNIA: I could even pull your body back to a building. So it'll be covered—

JOE: No, don't do that. I'm too heavy; you'd never be able to lift me.

PHRISKEDANNIA: Sure I could! I am not so weak. *(Stands up and points offstage right.)* I think   there is an old house about a mile that way...

JOE: Honest, Danny, don't worry about it.

PHRISKEDANNIA: OK, Joe.

(Pause. PHRISKEDANNIA sits down.)

JOE: Do you want me to drag you somewhere?

PHRISKEDANNIA: No, thank you.

JOE: I mean you brought it up. I could, it's no problem.

PHRISKEDANNIA: No, no. *(Motioning with hands.)* The jacket, the... phone call, that's fine. I'm not worried.

JOE: You sure? I don't want to—

PHRISKEDANNIA: Yes. I'm sure.

(Pause.)

PHRISKEDANNIA: Just from curiosity, are you religious, Joe?

JOE: No, not really. What about you?

PHRISKEDANNIA: Not especially. I—I believe in something, I think. But not all those church things.

JOE: That's good. I was worried I was gonna have to learn how to do Balvissian last rites.

PHRISKEDANNIA: *(laughs)* No. And for you, I just say, "He was a good ol' boy."

JOE: Do me a favor. Don't say that.

PHRISKEDANNIA: OK, then, I won't.

(*Pause. PHRISKEDANNIA stands up.*)

PHRISKEDANNIA: I know how to decide this.
JOE: Please don't tell me you've had another idea.

(*PHRISKEDANNIA reaches into his jacket pocket. Conscious that JOE will be nervous about this, he does so slowly and cautiously, looking at JOE. JOE says nothing. PHRISKEDAN-NIA pulls out a coin.*)

JOE: You mean…?
PHRISKEDANNIA: A throw of a coin. It's the only fair way.

(*Pause as JOE considers this.*)

PHRISKEDANNIA: You don't like it?
JOE: Don't you think it's a little…I mean, one of us is gonna die because of a coin toss? This is how they start the Super Bowl. It's not how people get killed.
PHRISKEDANNIA: Of course it's unusual. But we're in an unusual situation. (*pause*) It's just an idea. If you have a better idea, please let me know.

(*Pause. JOE stands up, stretches his neck.*)

JOE: It'll do, I guess.
PHRISKEDANNIA: In a way, it's civilized.
JOE: That explains why I never cared much for civility.
PHRISKEDANNIA: If you don't like it, say no.
JOE: No, no, this way's fine. Let's do it.
PHRISKEDANNIA: (*enthusiastically*) OK.

(PHRISKEDANNIA is about to toss the coin; JOE grabs the coin frantically just as it leaves his hand.)

JOE: Wait, will you? We haven't even chosen sides yet!

PHRISKEDANNIA: We choose sides when the coin is in the air. That way you know I am not cheating.

JOE: I haven't even seen the coin!

PHRISKEDANNIA: *(sarcastic)* Are you a coin collector? I keep learning new things about you, Joe.

JOE: Just let me see the coin first.

PHRISKEDANNIA: Open your hand then.

(JOE looks at the coin in his hand.)

JOE: *(Inspecting it.)* What's this thing?

PHRISKEDANNIA: It's a horse. A horse with wings. They don't really exist, but it's a sign of inspiration for our country. It is a symbol of—

JOE: Yeah, yeah, I know, a unicorn. So is this heads or tails?

PHRISKEDANNIA: What is that word, please?

JOE: Unicorn. *(Sounding it out, impatient.)* U-ni-corn. *(Flips the coin.)* So is this your fearless leader?

PHRISKEDANNIA: Unicorn. I never knew you had a word for it. In Balvissian we say, "Beddiappi". The famous horse with wings.

JOE: That's great, Danny. Now can we get back to the whole…coin toss situation?

PHRISKEDANNIA: Of course, of course. Please excuse me. I am fond of these horse…unicorns, so I am happy to have learned something from you.

JOE: Oh, wait a second. Pegasus.

PHRISKEDANNIA: Excuse me?

JOE: It's Pegasus, not unicorn. I'm getting my imaginary horses confused. Unicorns are the ones with the big horns on their head.

PHRISKEDANNIA: A horse with horns?

JOE: Just one.

PHRISKEDANNIA: Only one? Where?

JOE: *(pointing at his forehead)* A big long one. Right here.

PHRISKEDANNIA: A horse with a big, long, pointy thing. Everything is sex with you Americans.

JOE: Hey, it wasn't our idea.

PHRISKEDANNIA: Yes, but you probably imagined the horn longer and stronger, knowing you.

JOE: If it's an American unicorn, its horn *is* longer and stronger.

PHRISKEDANNIA: Very funny.

JOE: *(holding up coin)* So this guy?

PHRISKEDANNIA: Our leader, yes.

JOE: He looks a lot uglier in the photos we got.

PHRISKEDANNIA: Don't say this to my superiors, but I think your country's impression of him may be correct. I met him at a state dinner and he was…polite, but also very, very cold. It was something in his eyes that made me not comfortable. I tell you, I do not like him.

JOE: Hey, at least you got to meet the guy. The closest I got to *my* fearless leader was when the Kleenex ran out and I had to blow my nose on the newspaper.

PHRISKEDANNIA: I've seen him on television. He also looks like a typical politician.

JOE: I'm sure he is. I didn't vote for him.

PHRISKEDANNIA: Who did you vote for?

JOE: I don't vote.

PHRISKEDANNIA: But don't you work for the American democracy?

JOE: That's right.

PHRISKEDANNIA: But you don't vote?

JOE: I work to make sure people, all around the world, can vote. I'm told people like to do that. Me, I never much cared for it.

PHRISKEDANNIA: But don't you want to decide who becomes your president?

JOE: Are you kidding? I'd love to decide. I've got a couple of friends I think would be great for the role. But me voting isn't gonna get them elected.

PHRISKEDANNIA: Then the great American democracy is crooked?

JOE: Not like that. All I mean is, if what they said was true, each vote making a difference and all that jazz—I mean if it really came down to my vote, and just my vote, getting one guy elected instead of another guy—well, they'd throw the election out. One single vote? Deciding the whole election? There'd be all these lawsuits, court decisions…well, you saw what happened over a couple of dimples.

PHRISKEDANNIA: Oh yes, that reminds me, what exactly is a 'chad'?

JOE: Trust me, you don't want to know. All I'm saying is, a million votes might count, sure, but one vote counts nada.

PHRISKEDANNIA: Joe, I would not feel so bad if I were you. Our last election got called off when one of the politicians blew up the other one.

JOE: Yeah, I know. Bummer. *(beat)* Anyway, this guy *(He holds coin near PHRISKEDANNIA's face.)* is heads, and the unicorn *(flipping coin)* is tails. Right?

PHRISKEDANNIA: I've never heard it called that before.

JOE: Pegasus. You know what I mean.

PHRISKEDANNIA: I meant 'heads and tails'. I have never heard of that.

JOE: Well, what do you call it?

PHRISKEDANNIA: Man and animal.

JOE: Let's call it heads and tails, OK? Otherwise we'll just confuse ourselves.

PHRISKEDANNIA: Why would I confuse myself? That's what I've always called it.

JOE: You'll confuse me. So compromise a little.

PHRISKEDANNIA: But I am the one who's comprising. I could be using Balvissian, and calling it "Djaitos" and "Krepophki".

JOE: Look, this is your idea, and your coin. At least let me pick the language.

PHRISKEDANNIA: OK, OK. It doesn't matter—you get to pick your side, when the coin is in the air.

(Pause. PHRISKEDANNIA gets ready to throw.)

PHRISKEDANNIA: Heads and tails. Are you ready, Joe?

JOE: Ready, Danny.

(Pause.)

PHRISKEDANNIA: Heads and tails. You choose. Winning side touches the ground.

(Pause. PHRISKEDANNIA throws coin. JOE, registering what PHRISKEDANNIA has said, grabs coin from air wildly.)

JOE: *(losing his cool)* "Touches the ground?" What do you mean, "touches the ground"?

PHRISKEDANNIA: If you keep taking that coin out of the air I'm going to have a heart attack. That would solve our problem. Not very fair, I think, but it would solve our problem.

JOE: You're the one who said "touches the ground." Don't blame me for any of this.

PHRISKEDANNIA: What's wrong with touching the ground?

JOE: It's side *up*. Heads or tails, and whichever side is *up* wins—not touching the ground.

PHRISKEDANNIA: That is not how we do it in Balvissia.

JOE: *(yelling)* I don't care how we do it in Balvissia!

PHRISKEDANNIA: *(interrupting JOE, also yelling)* I don't care either! Let me throw the coin!

    (Pause, both looking at each other, veins out, in fighting stance. Gradually, their anger subsides and they smile.)

JOE: Man! This is hard work!

PHRISKEDANNIA: Now we know what they do in United Nations!

JOE: When they're not dining out in five-star restaurants, you mean. Let's sit down and work this thing out.

    (Both sit facing each other, cross-legged, on the floor.)

PHRISKEDANNIA: Coin.

JOE: *(handing coin in his hand to PHRISKEDANNIA.)* This coin.

    (PHRISKEDANNIA puts coin on ground between them.)

PHRISKEDANNIA: This coin. Throw-person.

JOE: You throw.

PHRISKEDANNIA: *(shakes head)* I think you should throw.

JOE: I can't. *(He holds his forearm.)* I got a cramp in my arm.

PHRISKEDANNIA: *(smiling)* I wish you told me that before our gunfight.

JOE: I can use it if I have to. I just don't want to aggravate it.

PHRISKEDANNIA: So I am throw-person.

JOE: Yep.

PHRISKEDANNIA: That means you call.

JOE: Unless you particularly want to call. I could always throw lefty—

PHRISKEDANNIA: I will throw. You—will call. Agreed?

JOE: Agreed.

PHRISKEDANNIA: Fine. Words.

JOE: Heads and tails?

PHRISKEDANNIA: Heads and tails.

JOE: You want those words I can't pronounce, don't you?

PHRISKEDANNIA: Not if you can't pronounce them. That would be the worst thing—I throw the coin up, but I can't hear what you say. Can you imagine?

JOE: I'd rather not.

PHRISKEDANNIA: Heads and tails. Now. Is anything forgotten?

JOE: That whole 'touching the ground' thing.

PHRISKEDANNIA: Yes. Your way is winning side is up.

JOE: Let's do it your way. Winning side is down.

PHRISKEDANNIA: No, I have the coin, and the throw. You only have the words.

JOE: Only because I gave you the throw. And I got the call.

PHRISKEDANNIA: Aha! *You* got the call. So you should pick your way, because you have to choose.

JOE: I choose winning side down.

PHRISKEDANNIA: Why? Why not your way?

JOE: *(Shrugs.)* Variety?

PHRISKEDANNIA: Whatever you say. OK, we are ready?

(JOE thinks for a moment.)

JOE: Ready.

(PHRISKEDANNIA gets up, dusts himself off. JOE also gets up, more slowly. They stare at each other for a couple of moments. PHRISKEDANNIA extends his arm, ready to throw. Finally, PHRISKEDANNIA throws the coin in the air. As it comes

down, however, PHRISKEDANNIA changes his mind and grabs it out of the air.)

JOE: *(exasperated)* What? What?

PHRISKEDANNIA: I forgot something.

JOE: *(calmer)* What?

PHRISKEDANNIA: Let's just get things clear. For instance, you say, "heads", and it is "heads"—on the ground, I mean, heads are down—then you kill me, right?

JOE: Right.

PHRISKEDANNIA: And you call, "heads", and it's…tails—then I kill you, right?

JOE: Right.

PHRISKEDANNIA: And the same will follow for tails—only backwards, you understand…

JOE: *(impatiently)* Right, right.

PHRISKEDANNIA: Ok, fine.

(PHRISKEDANNIA gets ready to throw. JOE, upset at the delay, slaps his forehead in exasperation. PHRISKEDANNIA stops to explain.)

PHRISKEDANNIA: Because it could be, if you call it right, you die. I was not sure. I just want everything to be clear.

(JOE gently grabs PHRISKEDANNIA's throwing arm.)

JOE: *(slowly, making sure he doesn't get it wrong)* If I call heads, I die on…tails down, you die on heads down. If I call tails, I die on…heads down, and you die on tails down. Is that right?

PHRISKEDANNIA: *(beat)* Yes, that sounds like what we agreed. We should have written this down.

JOE: *(Spreads arms in a shrug.)* No pen.

PHRISKEDANNIA: Me neither. Ready?

(JOE nods.)

PHRISKEDANNIA: Good luck.

(PHRISKEDANNIA throws the coin.)

JOE: Heads!

(The coin lands. They both look at each other, and approach the coin. They both—though we cannot—observe the upside. They trade glances again, and then PHRISKEDANNIA—even though they both know what will be revealed—flips the coin over and holds it in his palm. They look at each other. PHRISKEDANNIA pockets the coin. JOE sits down. PHRISKEDANNIA walks stage right several steps, then looks out at something in that direction. He walks back and sits on JOE's right.)

JOE: Cigarette?

PHRISKEDANNIA: No, thanks.

JOE: Mind if I have one?

PHRISKEDANNIA: Please do.

(JOE takes out cigarette and lights it. Pause.)

PHRISKEDANNIA: In my country they say, *(in Balvissian)* "Djaitai kolai-nerr dokhai fattan ava sollostre." The best time to die is at the end of your life.

JOE: That's convenient.

PHRISKEDANNIA: It sounds stupid, I know. It's hard to explain—maybe it does not translate well. All it means is—live completely, the way that you want to, so when you die—it will have been your life. Sorry, does that make any sense?

JOE: Yeah, I got it.

PHRISKEDANNIA: Do you agree?

JOE: *(beat)* Yeah, I think so.

> *(PHRISKEDANNIA stands and taps both JOE's shoulders with his finger, as though knighting him.)*

PHRISKEDANNIA: Then I appoint you an honorary Balvissian.

JOE: I'm touched.

> *(PHRISKEDANNIA turns and walks towards jackets.)*

PHRISKEDANNIA: And now we have something to do.

> *(PHRISKEDANNIA puts his jacket on. Reaching into his pocket, he pulls out the gun.)*

PHRISKEDANNIA: This is the right time.

> *(Pause.)*

JOE: I don't know about that. But I guess it's the best time we've got.

> *(PHRISKEDANNIA hands the gun to JOE, barrel pointing towards himself. JOE points the gun at PHRISKEDANNIA from where he sits. After a pause, PHRISKEDANNIA touches JOE on his left arm.)*

PHRISKEDANNIA: Nice to meet you.

(Pause.)

PHRISKEDANNIA: Aren't you going to shoot me? I don't have all day.

JOE: Do you want to try running or something? I can't shoot you like this.

PHRISKEDANNIA: You'd rather shoot me in the back?

JOE: You bet I would. Come on, I'll give you a head start. I won't shoot until you get to that tree.

PHRISKEDANNIA: Are you a good shot?

JOE: So-so.

PHRISKEDANNIA: You're just saying that to make me feel better.

JOE: Will you run?

PHRISKEDANNIA: OK, OK, I'll run. If it's easier for you, I'll run.

(Pause.)

PHRISKEDANNIA: You won't forget about the jacket?

JOE: No. I'll make sure I tie it around your face, like you said.

PHRISKEDANNIA: Thank you.

JOE: Don't mention it.

PHRISKEDANNIA: Okay. (beat) Won't you aggravate your arm?

JOE: My arm?

PHRISKEDANNIA: When you shoot me.

JOE: Yeah, a little bit, I guess.

PHRISKEDANNIA: You can't shoot left-handed?

JOE: Naw, not well. But I'll be all right.

PHRISKEDANNIA: I am glad to hear it.

JOE: Thanks, buddy.

(Pause. JOE steps on his cigarette and stands up.)

PHRISKEDANNIA: You will shoot me, right?

JOE: I don't know. I'll certainly aim at you. After that, I'm not sure. I guess with you further away, it might feel like target practice. That'd make it easier.

PHRISKEDANNIA: Good luck. I almost hope that you do shoot me. If I get away, it's too—Hollywood.

JOE: Would you prefer drowning next to Kate Winslet?

PHRISKEDANNIA: *(laughs)* Very much, but we have neither ocean nor actress.

(Pause.)

PHRISKEDANNIA: Well, I don't mean to be rude, but I must be going.

JOE: Listen, Danny—Phriskedannia...

(Beat.)

JOE: It really has been nice meeting you. I don't want you to think that—any of this...

PHRISKEDANNIA: As they say in my country, "Life is a game of a chess, or it is not. In either instance, play chess."

JOE: *(in Balvissian)* Keliadda botuzzi grascht; grascht hakkan. Okhai undelascht, botuzzi brechen.

PHRISKEDANNIA: You do speak Balvissian!

(Joe holds thumb and finger close to signify 'a little'.)

JOE: *(in Balvissian)* Antorecht.

PHRISKEDANNIA: You liar!

JOE: I know. I'm sorry.

PHRISKEDANNIA: Do not be sorry. I am not sorry.

(PHRISKEDANNIA clasps JOE's left hand.)

PHRISKEDANNIA: Today has been a very good day.

(Pause. Then PHRISKEDANNIA, almost playfully, runs off, yelling. A few seconds later, JOE raises his gun.)

CURTAIN

Alivelike Cohen,
Goodlike Bukowski

◆

The Normandy fields were everywhere
that summer.
And we had stopped at a *station-service* to pick up an old Bob Dylan
because any more of Phil's Weird Al cassette
would drive us all crazy.

I was just fifteen then and had not yet learned, had not yet
needed to know, what it meant
to be alive.

Bob Dylan spoke a foreign tongue.
He sang the Normandy cornfields
and the sound of road
and the things you could never possibly
speak about.

Ted had this stuffed lamb
called Lamby or something,
that looked worn

from day one, and was loved into
a straggly, angelic mess.

Back in Connecticut, I'd
listen to "Greatest Hits, Volume 2",
late under the covers,
until sleep overcame me.

About the Author

———————◆———————

Bob Janis has lived in Boston, England, and Connecticut, and has held every position that befits a struggling writer: coffee shop barista, marketing coordinator, philosophy undergraduate, paralegal, church worker, fruit stand attendant, local journalist, community access television director, and substitute teacher. *Displicit* is his first book. He can be reached at ilovedisplicit@yahoo.com.

0-595-22316-8